**sony pictures**
**Animation**

# SMURFS™

## THE LOST VILLAGE

# SMURFS™

## THE LOST VILLAGE
### Movie Novelization

Adapted by Stacia Deutsch

Simon Spotlight
New York  London  Toronto  Sydney  New Delhi

SIMON SPOTLIGHT
An imprint of Simon & Schuster Children's Publishing Division
1230 Avenue of the Americas, New York, New York 10020
This Simon Spotlight edition February 2017
SMURFS™ & © Peyo 2017 Licensed through Lafig Belgium/IMPS. Smurfs: The Lost Village, the Movie © 2017 Columbia Pictures Industries, Inc. and LSC Film Corporation. All Rights Reserved.
All rights reserved, including the right of reproduction in whole or in part in any form.
SIMON SPOTLIGHT and colophon are registered trademarks of Simon & Schuster, Inc.
For information about special discounts for bulk purchases, please contact Simon & Schuster Special Sales at 1-866-506-1949 or business@simonandschuster.com.
Designed by Nick Sciacca
Manufactured in the United States of America 0117 OFF
10 9 8 7 6 5 4 3 2 1
ISBN 978-1-4814-8103-8
ISBN 978-1-4814-8104-5 (eBook)

# Chapter 1

"Many great adventures usually start somewhere interesting. Case in point: This one begins in a secret place hidden deep in the forest. Welcome to Smurf Village, where all the Smurfs live happily in their quaint mushroom houses." Papa Smurf looked up from the book he was holding and turned toward the window, where Smurf Village was bustling with activity. "Oh, what's a Smurf you ask? Well, how about a little background."

Just then, a Smurf came barreling into town, bumping into anything and anyone in his path.

Here was the perfect example. "So *this* is a Smurf. Tiny, blue, funny hat. And they look pretty darn good in a pair of white tights. What does a Smurf do? Just ask him his name. For instance, his name is Clumsy," Papa said with a knowing grin.

"Hi!" Clumsy waved, not watching where he was going. It was no surprise when he tripped, tumbled, and fell into a hollowed-out log.

"I'm okay!" Clumsy's voice echoed through the village.

With a small chuckle and shake of his head, Papa Smurf went on with his introductions.

"Then there's Jokey Smurf and Gullible Smurf . . ."

Jokey Smurf handed Gullible Smurf a gift box. "Present for you!" exclaimed Jokey. Suddenly, the box exploded, and Jokey burst into laughter.

"Just kidding. I meant to give you this one," he said, producing another box.

"Wow, thanks!" Gullible accepted the present happily, but when he opened the box, a boxing glove sprang out and punched him in the face.

Across town, Hefty Smurf was doing push-ups. "Ninety-eight, ninety-nine . . . one hundred!" he grunted, kissing his big arm muscles. "And now for the one-fingered push-ups!"

"And over here is Nerdy Smurf," Papa said as a Smurf rode by on a scooter.

"Excuse me?" the Smurf shot back.

2

"Sorry, Brainy. Just kidding!" Brainy got back on his scooter. "There's also Mime Smurf and Instigator Smurf."

"Watch this," Instigator Smurf said with a mischievous grin. "Hey! Look out!" he called to Mime Smurf.

Mime Smurf suddenly collided with an invisible wall.

"Hmm . . . what's going on over there?" Nosey Smurf wondered aloud.

Nosey Smurf was watching everything through binoculars. He checked out Paranoid Smurf, who quickly closed his window blinds.

"There's also Winner Smurf and Loser . . . ," Papa said, gesturing to two Smurfs playing checkers. Winner Smurf was about to celebrate when Loser Smurf flipped the chessboard over in a fit of rage.

"Karate Smurf." Papa waved to a Smurf who kicked Gullible Smurf in the stomach.

Handy Smurf pounded nails.

Vanity Smurf admired himself in his mirror.

Farmer Smurf plucked radishes from his garden.

Painter put the finishing touches on his masterpiece.

Baker Smurf set out a cake to cool.

Magician Smurf made the cake disappear.

And there were even more: Scuba Smurf, Policeman Smurf, Therapist Smurf, Table-Eating Smurf . . .

Papa Smurf paused at Table-Eating Smurf and admitted, "Yeah, we're not too sure about him either." He shrugged, saying, "And then there's me—Papa Smurf. I rock the red tights." Papa chuckled so hard his belly shook. Then suddenly stopped. "But this story isn't about me. And it isn't about them. It's about *her.*"

Outside, a Smurf with long blond hair, wearing a white dress, passed by Papa's window.

"Smurfette," Papa said with a fond smile. "The only girl in our village."

The other Smurfs cheerfully greeted Smurfette as she wandered through town.

"Hey, Laundry Smurf!" Smurfette waved at him, then at the next group of Smurfs she saw. "Hey, guys!"

Papa leaned back in his chair. "But that's not the only thing different about Smurfette," he explained. "She was created by the evil wizard, Gargamel.

With the help of dark magic, he made Smurfette from a lump of clay."

High above Smurf Village there was a run-down castle on the side of a rocky mountain. The hovel was isolated, and the weather there was always terrible. The dark sky was filled with lightning blasts and thunderous roars.

Inside the shadowy ruin, the evil wizard had molded blue clay into a small Smurf-form. With a whip of his wand, he used dark magic to bring the clay form to life.

*BAM!*

A moonbeam zapped the clay form, and an evil Smurfette rose from the smoke. This Smurfette was nothing like the one who lived in Smurf Village now. This one had a sinister smile.

Papa Smurf shivered. "At first, she was as bad as him. He sent her to find Smurf Village and help him capture us all."

Evil Smurfette had entered the village with only one goal: She was there to cause trouble.

"Luckily, I also know a little magic of my own and was able to find the good in Smurfette and help her to shine," Papa said.

Good Smurfette took a little while to fit in, but once she did, she was everyone's friend.

Papa rested his hand on the storybook that was still sitting on his lap. "But there was still one problem. Smurfette's name doesn't tell us anything about her."

Smurfette had tried chemistry with Brainy, and that hadn't ended well. Brainy ended up falling down a hole! She tried karate, with Karate Smurf as her mentor, but when she kicked him . . . Well, let's just say a kick while wearing high heels can really hurt!

"Her name doesn't tell us who she is or what she does. So, what exactly is a Smurfette?"

That was a big question. Everyone wanted to know the answer.

Smurfette tried baking a cake with Baker Smurf, but the cake crumbled. Baker Smurf reported, "Well, she's not a baker, I can tell you that for sure."

Brainy Smurf brought out a guide to Smurfs from his extensive library and started flipping through it. "Hmm, let's see. Smurfette . . . Smurfette . . . Huh, it's not here."

"You know . . . A Smurfette's, uh . . ." Handy Smurf didn't have a clue.

6

Farmer Smurf was equally flummoxed. "Well, golly, that's a tough one."

Mime Smurf only shrugged.

"What's a Smurfette?" Postal Smurf mulled over the answer. "Well, she's, uh, she's . . . hmmm."

Hefty Smurf had the answer. He smiled as he said, "She's just the greatest. . . ."

Vanity Smurf was still staring at himself in the mirror when he added, "The most wondrous creature on Earth! Yes, you are!" He meant himself, not Smurfette. "I'm sorry, what was the question?"

"Smurfette? Um . . . Oh! I got it!" Clumsy was one of her best friends. He said, "This is one of those eternal questions that we'll never *ever* know the answer to!" Unbeknownst to Clumsy, Smurfette had heard them all wondering about her. It made Smurfette sad.

After much thought, Papa reiterated the question, "So, what is a Smurfette?" He shrugged. "No one wanted to know the answer to that question more than Smurfette herself. . . ."

Jazzy Smurf played a sad tune while Smurfette wandered over to a bench and sat down. She sighed as she watched the world go by.

"Eh, what are you doing?" Grouchy Smurf stood by the bench, hovering over her.

"Oh, hey Grouchy. I was just—"

"Leaving," he suggested.

"Uhhhh . . ." That wasn't actually her plan.

"This is my bench. I come here at the *same* time every day and—"

"Ohh, let me guess . . . ," she interrupted. "You grouch."

"Yeah."

Smurfette moved over so he could sit down next to her.

"I can do that. I can grouch." She tried to use his same voice and tone.

Random Smurf came up to them. "Hey, Grouchy. Hey, Smurfette! Nice day, huh?"

"NO IT'S NOT!" Grouchy was being his best self.

"IT'S GONNA RAAAAAIIIINNNNN!!" Smurfette grumped, but it didn't come out sounding right. She wasn't a naturally grouchy person. In her own voice, she added, "Which actually helps the plants grow!" She tried again. "But also means it's gonna be cloudy! So chew on that!" Then, "But then again, there might be a rainbow!" It was so hard to stay grouchy! "But rainbows are dumb!"

Smurfette shook her head. She just couldn't do it. "Just kidding, I love rainbows! GAHHH!!"

"You're not very good at this, are you?" Grouchy Smurf asked with a grouchy sigh.

"Uh, no I'm not," she admitted.

"In fact, you're actually kinda bad at it." Grouchy Smurf was still the only grouch in town.

"Yup." Smurfette started to leave, but then she stopped and turned back. "But you're also bad at it!" Oh that was awful. "That's a lie! You're really, really good at it!"

In the end, only one thing was certain: Smurfette still didn't know what it meant to be a Smurfette!

# Chapter 2

Smurfette went to Brainy's mushroom. She was about to knock on the door when Brainy Smurf popped out. He was wearing a lab coat, looking frazzled.

"Hi, Brainy!" Smurfette was happy to see him.

Brainy coughed. "Ahh, Smurfette! Thank goodness you're here!" He leaned past her, glanced around nervously, and grabbed her arm, dragging her inside.

Smurfette began to protest. "I was just—Whoa!" In Brainy's lab, Hefty Smurf was sitting in a chair. On his head was a ridiculous hat made from an old spaghetti colander and some root vegetables. It was connected by wires to a machine that rattled and hummed.

"We're running trials on my new invention, the Smurfy Thing Finder. Test subject: Hefty Smurf," Clumsy explained to her.

"Hey, Smurfette." Hefty waved.

"Uh . . . hey. That thing's safe, right?" Smurfette whispered to Brainy. She became even more worried when she saw Brainy duck behind a blast shield for protection.

"Is it safe?" Brainy brushed her worry away. "Psshh. Of course." He paused, took a deep breath, and warned her, "I'd get back here if I were you."

Smurfette considered what to do, then decided to join Brainy behind the blast shield, leaving Hefty on his own. Brainy recorded the experiment with his Snappy Bug. It was the Smurf equivalent to a smartphone, but it was also an actual ladybug.

"Snappy Bug, take this down. Smurfy Thing Finder, Trial 1.03." He looked up and asked, "Ready, Hefty?"

"Roger that!" Hefty gave a thumbs-up.

The contraption powered up, set to full throttle. There were a series of scientific beeps and whistles while a string of lights glowed between the helmet and a prognosis dial. The dial spun wildly before stopping on an icon. It was a picture of a big arm muscle.

"Whoa!" Smurfette gasped.

"Ha-ha! It works!" Brainy cheered.

Snappy Bug celebrated too.

"Wow! This thing really gets me," Hefty said, flexing his arm.

Brainy told Smurfette, "It's able to hone in on Hefty's dominant trait—"

"Superstrength!" Hefty said joyfully, kissing his bicep.

"Which I distill into this," Brainy held up a drink can. "I call it Brainy's Super Smurfy Power Fuel." He passed the can to Smurfette. "Here. You can try it first!"

Smurfette examined the drink, uncertain if she should try it.

Rushing away from her and the can, Brainy leaped behind the protective blast shield. "All clear!" he shouted, meaning she should drink up.

Smurfette shook her head. "Yeah, see, when you say things like 'all clear,' it make me *not* want to drink it."

The mushroom door flung open as Clumsy burst into the room.

"Hey, guys!" He knocked the drink right out of Smurfette's hand and *BOOM*! It exploded, leaving a gaping and smoking hole in the wall.

Whew! Smurfette was glad she didn't drink it!

"Hi, Clumsy," they all said together.

"You're just in time to witness scientific history," Brainy began. Looking up, he noticed that through the hole left by the blast, Nosey Smurf was casually strolling by, slowing taking in what had happened.

"What's going on in here?" Nosey said, nosing around.

Brainy, Hefty, Smurfette, and Clumsy all told him, "None of your business, Nosey!"

"Hmmm, well, all right." Nosey wasn't offended. He simply continued on his way.

Suddenly, Smurfette had an idea! Maybe now she could finally learn what her name meant! "Hey! If that vegetable hat can tell us that Hefty is strong, maybe it can tell me what an 'ette' is." She rushed forward and put on the odd helmet. "Power it up, Brainy!"

The boys gathered behind the blast shield as Brainy powered up the machine.

Brainy flipped a switch, and another series of scientific beeps, whistles, and lights went off until the machine started to spark and smoke. It was shaking. The whole mushroom house rumbled. Candles blew out. All of Brainy's furniture was magnetically pulled toward Smurfette until finally the contraption sputtered to a stop, causing the vegetables on the helmet to wither and wilt.

"Whoa!" Brainy exclaimed, coming out from behind the barrier. "Fascinating!"

"What happened?!" Smurfette was baffled. Why didn't it work like it did for Hefty?

"Somehow, instead of sending energy out, you absorbed it. Probably something to do with the fact that you're not a real—" Slamming a hand over his mouth, Brainy stopped talking.

Smurfette threw down the helmet. "A real Smurf? Go ahead, you can say it."

Brainy immediately said, "No! I just meant this machine wasn't built for a Smurf of your, well, origins."

"Yeah, it's okay. I get it." Smurfette was upset.

Hefty tried to lighten the mood. "Hey, you know what? Let's all go have some fun!"

That made Smurfette feel a little better. "Yeah!" she said, allowing them to distract her. It would be nice to have a day out. But what should they do?

Hefty, Brainy, and Smurfette all agreed. "Smurfboarding!"

"Pizza!" Clumsy said at the same time. "I mean smurfboarding!

# Chapter
# 3

While Brainy was trying out his invention, the evil wizard Gargamel was in his craggy hovel, working on his own creation.

"It's almost ready, Azrael." Gargamel mixed a potion in his cauldron while his nasty sidekick cat was busy looking out at the forest through a telescope. He ignored Gargamel—like usual.

"A pinch of newt poo, a gram of calcified fungus from between the toes of a yak, and a piece of cheese I left in my underpants last week!" Gargamel took the chunk of cheese from his robe and ate a bite before adding it to the cauldron. "That oughta do it."

The cauldron began to sizzle, and a moment later, the spell was complete. Using long tongs, he removed an orb from the boiling cauldron and placed it in an egg carton with other sizzling orbs.

Gargamel was pleased. "Presto! Twelve spherical petrification modules." He rotated one for a better look. "Or as I like to call 'em: Freeze Balls!"

Just for fun, Gargamel tossed one at a mouse that was scurrying across the floor. It struck the rodent, which became frozen and motionless. It squeaked in horror.

"You're welcome, Azrael." Gargamel rubbed his hands together. "Dinner is served."

"Meow!" Azrael rejected the gift.

"Ingrate!" the wizard spat, then decided he didn't care what the cat thought. "Besides, these Freeze Balls aren't for catching mice!" Gargamel used a skull to project hand-drawn images of Smurfs up onto the wall. "They're for capturing those elusive Smurfs! My holy grail . . . The gold at the end of my rainbow . . ." Gargamel clicked through a presentation he'd prepared. "Their essence is the most potent magical ingredient in the world! Next slide."

The next image was of hundreds of Smurfs, a plus sign, and a cauldron.

"Imagine the power in a hundred of them combined!" Gargamel went to the next slide.

Azrael suddenly got very excited. He noticed something through the telescope and tried to get Gargamel's attention. "Meow, meow, MEOW!"

"Not now, Azrael! I'm in a middle of a lecture!" The wizard went on saying, "My plan is simple." He rapidly flipped through slide after slide. "Find Smurf Village. Capture all the Smurfs. Drain them of their magic. And finally, use that magic to become the most powerful wizard in the world! Mwahahahaha!"

Gargamel stepped in front of the screen, the on-screen image of himself with hair shone over his own bald head.

"Ooooh, look at me with hair!" he gushed.

"Meow, meow, MEOW!" Azrael was frantic. "Meow, meow, MEOW!"

Finally, Gargamel took notice. "What? Why didn't you say so in the first place?" He dashed over and knocked Azrael off the stool.

"MEOW!" Azrael complained.

Gargamel peered out and was surprised to see four Smurfs climbing to the top of a hill in the distance. "Blue blazes, I've spotted Smurfs in the forest!"

Azrael growled, offended by the lack of respect,

since *he* was the one who had seen them first.

The wizard growled back. "Well, it's MY telescope. . . ."

He called to his vulture who was at the garbage can picking through leftover scraps. "Monty! Come, my majestic eagle!"

The vulture landed on Gargamel's shoulder, causing him to cry out in pain while swatting at the bird. "Oooh— Ahh— Ouch. Your talons are digging into my shoulders!" Monty loosened his grip slightly. "Yes, that's better." Gargamel pointed at the forest. "Now fly! Go capture me some Smurfs!"

Gargamel gave Monty a small push out the window. The bird took off—

"No, no! You're going the wrong way!" Gargamel called with a sigh.

Turning back, Monty adjusted his flight path and headed off toward the unsuspecting Smurfs.

Hefty, Brainy, Clumsy, and Smurfette—or "Team Smurf" as they called themselves—arrived at the mountaintop, holding their smurfboards. They looked down at the course below. Hefty tossed his board over the edge and jumped onto it like a pro. "Whoa!! Yeah!!" he cheered as he soared through the air and stuck an awesome landing.

It was Brainy's turn next. He showed off his new streamlined smurfboard, but he had some technical difficulties midair.

"Oh no!" Brainy exclaimed as he fell out of the sky and landed in Hefty's arms. "I guess I should've packed a parachute."

Clumsy was ready to roll. He harnessed himself into a barrel for protection on all sides. "My turn! Safety third!"

"Oh boy," Brainy and Hefty said at the same time, ducking for cover.

"Whoa, whoa, whoa!" The barrel bounced off course and sent Clumsy flying. "AHHHHHHH!" Crashing out of a bush, zooming past Brainy and Hefty, Clumsy ran smack into a tree trunk and landed with a thud!

"WOOOO-HOOOOOO!"

While the others helped Clumsy, they looked up to see Smurfette flying above them, using leaves as wings.

"Wow," Hefty said, admiring how she soared. "Really takes your breath away, doesn't she?"

"This is incredible!" Smurfette was about to land when a gust of wind caught her leaf-wings. "Whoa! Uh-oh!" She was being blown off course, heading for trouble.

"Oh no! She's getting way too close to the Forbidden Forest!" Brainy shouted.

"She can't go over that wall! Come on!" Hefty led the others. They ran as fast as they could after her.

"Whoooooaa! Oof!" Smurfette landed with a thud on the ground by the big stone boundary to the Forbidden Forest.

She stood, but she had the eerie feeling she was being watched. Glancing around nervously, something caught her eye in a nearby bush. What was it? She looked closer.

Suddenly, there were eyes staring right back at her. The creature was camouflaged by the bush, but they each stared into the other's eyes for a long beat before the creature took off running.

"No, no, no, wait! Don't go! Wait, wait! Who are you? Don't be afraid!" Smurfette called after it.

As it fled, Smurfette noticed something: The

creature was a Smurf! How was that possible?!

She chased the new Smurf all the way to a wall, where he dashed through a small hole into the Forbidden Forest.

"Hey! No! You can't go in there!" Smurfette called after him. She didn't dare enter the forest and skidded to a stop. The Smurf disappeared, but beside the hole, there was a tiny tan hat he had left behind. Smurfette was studying it when the boys arrived, out of breath and worried.

They all talked at once:

"Smurfette!"

"You okay?!"

"What happened?!"

Smurfette blurted out, "I saw a Smurf!"

"What?!" Brainy didn't believe her.

"Who was it?" Clumsy wanted to know.

"I don't know, I couldn't get a good look, but he was wearing this!" She held up the hat. She was about to say more, when suddenly—

"Ca-CAW!"

Gargamel's huge bird appeared, and with a mighty whoosh, he snatched Smurfette up and tossed her into a burlap sack.

"Smurfette! Code blue! Guys, c'mon!" Hefty gave chase.

Inside the sack, Smurfette put up an angry fight, fists flying, legs kicking, struggling to break free, but it was no use.

Hefty ran fast and lunged for Monty, getting a hold of his feathers right before he lifted off.

Clumsy and Brainy launched rocks and Smurfberries at the bird, trying to knock him down.

The bird flew strong, and even Hefty was unable to hold on. With a thud, he fell to the ground. And Smurfette was carried away!

Hefty, Brainy, and Clumsy exchanged terrified looks as Hefty announced, "We gotta get her!"

The Smurfs sprinted after Smurfette as she was carried toward Gargamel's wretched cliffside hovel.

"I have a baaaad feeling about this," Clumsy said, his voice shaking.

"Oh, do you? Does it have to do with the giant vulture carrying our friend off to Gargamel's lair?!" Brainy asked sarcastically.

"Smurfeeeeeette!" Hefty's voice echoed through the forest while their friend was delivered to the evil wizard.

# Chapter 4

Inside Gargamel's dark, ruined castle, the wizard and his cat awaited Monty's return.

Monty misjudged the opening and hit the windowsill with a tremendous crash before finding his way inside. Opening his talons, he dropped the burlap sack on a long worktable.

"Monty, my regal raptor, you've done it! You caught a Smurf?!" He leaned into the bird, lips pursed. "Give me a kiss!"

"Meow," Azrael groaned, rolling his eyes. It was disgusting.

Gargamel picked up the sack and paraded it across the room.

"Finally, you bring me what I've been asking for. A tiny, blue-skinned, shirtless—" He shoved the contents of the bag into a cage, only to realize the prisoner was Smurfette.

"YOU!" Gargamel shouted at her.

Azrael hissed!

"Let me outta here you—you Smurf-obsessed wannabe wizard!" She hid the strange Smurf hat that she'd found behind her back.

"Is that any way to treat the man who brought you into this world? I'd prefer it if you just called me Papa!" Gargamel put his face close to the cage.

"I would never call you that!" Smurfette protested. She had a papa, and it certainly wasn't Gargamel.

"Your loss!" He moved away. Then, turning to his bird, he said, "Nice catch, Monty! Unfortunately, *this* vile creature isn't even a real Smurf."

Smurfette accidentally dropped the Smurf hat. She snatched it up and then quickly shoved it behind her back again. Gargamel narrowed his eyes and leaned in.

"What's this?! What are you hiding?!" He shook the cage. "Hand it over, you pseudo-Smurf!" Gargamel reached through the bars, but Smurfette dodged his thick fingers.

She didn't notice that Azrael was behind her. The

mangy cat managed to nip the hat away from her.

"Thank you, Azrael," Gargamel said.

Azrael put up his paw for a high five, but Gargamel left him hanging. He was more interested in the odd object he was holding.

"What do have we here? Hmmm." Gargamel studied the hat under a magnifying glass.

"Meow. Meow," Azrael told him.

"A different design?" That made sense. "Yes, uh, of course. I noticed that right away! Slightly before you did, in fact!"

"Meow," Azrael grunted.

The wizard crossed back to Smurfette, determined to get the truth. "Where did you get it?!"

"I'm not telling you anything!" She crossed her arms over her chest.

"TELL ME!" he shouted.

"NO!"

"You better tell me!" he tried again in a stern voice.

Smurfette's answer was the same. "NO!"

"Fine, don't tell me!" Gargamel said, trying some reverse psychology . . .

But that didn't work on Smurfette. "I won't!"

"Who cares! You've already given me what I needed." Gargamel went to his cabinet and began rummaging through different potion bottles. "Come along, Azrael!"

Outside, Hefty, Clumsy, and Brainy had finally made their way up the mountainside and were peeking in through Azrael's cat door.

Hefty made military hand signals, but Brainy and Clumsy didn't understand them. He tried again.

Clumsy thought he had it all figured out. "Oh, I know this. Go left, then right, back handspring, stick the landing."

Hefty shook his head and tried again. "Is it a person, book, or movie?" Clumsy whispered.

Brainy knew this game of charades wasn't going to get them anywhere. He whispered, "No one ever understands your hand signals, Hefty!"

Frustrated, Hefty said, "Aggghhh! Never mind. Just follow me. And stay close."

The boys snuck across the floor and climbed up toward Smurfette.

Gargamel didn't notice them. He was obsessed with the hat. He pulled on a thread, which made the entire thing unravel. Which was what he wanted to do. Waving his hand over the threads, Gargamel began to chant.

"Wort of worm, and hair of cat," he intoned, sprinkling ingredients into a cauldron.

Azrael did a double take when he saw the hair. When had Gargamel taken a patch of fur off him?

"Show me the home of this Smurf hat!"

After all the ingredients were combined, there was a major magical reaction.

A disembodied voice boomed from the cauldron. "Long you have searched for these creatures of blue, but this hat comes from somewhere new."

Rubbing his hands together happily, Gargamel shouted, "Yes! Where?! Where does it come from?!"

The cauldron went on. "A village of Smurfs, where enchantment grows . . ."

This was better than Gargamel ever dreamed. "An entire village? Go on!"

"PLEASE STOP INTERRUPTING," the cauldron scolded.

"Okay, sorry. . . . Please continue."

"The location of which . . ."

The wizard bent in to make sure he heard the directions clearly. "Yes?"

"Nobody knows." That was the cauldron's final answer.

"NOOOOO!!! Just start with that! Start with 'I don't know'! Lousy, cheapo cauldron!" Gargamel kicked the big black pot, hurting himself in the process. "Ow-hoo-hoo-hoo!"

The kick made the cauldron speak again.

"But here is a clue. . . ."

The Smurf hat thread floated to the surface of the potion and began to form a shape.

"Fascinating. What is it? I've got it. Three finger puppets with really big, puffy hair!" Gargamel nodded as he considered the image.

"Mreow, mreow," Azrael said. They were obviously trees.

"Trees? Must be a symbol for something, or a code," he muttered to himself, trying to decipher the code. "Trees, trees, breeze, knees . . . Babies crawl on their knees! Check all the nurseries in the area!"

Azrael was already moving toward the map that was hanging on the wall.

Gargamel ignored him as he continued to plan. "We're going to need to disguise ourselves as babies. Now, where can I get a giant diaper?"

"Meow, meow, meow!" Azrael pointed, waving a paw frantically to a spot on the map.

Gargamel was annoyed. "Azrael, it's not your map. If you want your own map, we'll get you your own map! But this is *my* map. . . ." Just to get the cat to stop, he gave in and went to look. "Wait a minute. Look what I found." He pointed with his wand. "Three Tall Trees! In the Forbidden Forest."

Azrael rolled his eyes. He did all the work and never got any credit!

"We've never searched there before. I'm a genius! Azrael, it's time to take a road trip!"

Frustrated and annoyed, Azrael refused to help as the wizard began to pack a bag.

While Gargamel was distracted, the Smurfs worked quickly to pick the lock on Smurfette's cage. They didn't have much time. The wizard was dashing back and forth across the lab, preparing for his trip.

When Gargamel stopped at the cage, they had to rush to hide.

"Oh, Smurfette, congratulations! You've just led me to an undiscovered population of Smurfs!"

This was terrible! Smurfette shook her head.

"They have no idea we even exist!" Gargamel was so pleased. "I'll be like . . ." He pretended he was sneaking up and attacking.

"And they'll be all . . ." He made a surprised face.

"And I'll go . . ." He moved his hands, as if there was a mighty explosion.

"And then they'll be like . . ." He made a terrified expression. Then, with an echoing laugh, Gargamel leaned down, looking directly at Smurfette.

"At last, I'll have all the Smurfs I need to harness their magic and become infinitely more powerful! You little evil genius. The rotten apple doesn't fall too far from the tree after all." He smiled to himself and then went back to the map. "Get your fur and feathers in gear, boys!" Gargamel told Azrael and Monty. "We'll leave at first light, right after breakfast, say eight or eight thirty . . . nine at the latest!"

Gargamel then turned back to continue formulating his plot. That was Team Smurf's cue; they finally managed to bust the lock and set Smurfette free.

"Wait, Brainy—the map!" Smurfette whispered, and pointed.

31

"I'm on it," Brainy said with a wink. Using Snappy Bug, he took a bunch of photographs of the map on Gargamel's wall. They were going to need them.

Gargamel kept revising his schedule. "Barring any light packing and last-minute potty breaks . . ." He reevaluated the departure. "Fine, maybe nine thirty. Absolutely no later than ten, though!" Feeling satisfied, he rotated on his heel to see how his prisoner was doing, but the cage was empty!

"WHAT THE—" Gargamel's voice boomed.

There! Gargamel spotted Smurfette and the boys running for the window.

"It's a jailbreak!" he exclaimed. "No—they know my plans! They'll ruin everything!"

The Smurfs had to act fast. Hefty instructed the others to climb onto Gargamel's crossbow bolt.

"Is this safe?" Brainy asked.

"Well, it's a giant crossbow, so I'm gonna go with NO!" Hefty took a seat.

"Don't let them escape!" Gargamel shouted.

Azrael dashed across the room, claws drawn, anxious to catch the Smurfs.

Gargamel came at them from the other direction.

32

The Smurfs were cornered, but just when it seemed like they would surely be caught, the mouse that'd been frozen before returned for its revenge. It pushed a Freeze Ball off the shelf, which hit Gargamel, freezing him in midair.

The wizard couldn't move. "Get them! Get those Smurfs!" He told his minions.

"Uhhhh, where are the seat belts?!" Smurfette turned, wide-eyed, to Hefty.

He told her to hang on and then announced, "Fire in the hole!" And with that, he kicked the crossbow trigger hard. Team Smurf went sailing through the air, down the hall, and out the cat door.

Monty chased them. He flew out of the front of the lair but didn't make it far before he smacked into a fence door.

"GET THOSE SMURFS!" Gargamel was still frozen.

Azrael zoomed past Monty. He turned back briefly to see Monty's head stuck.

"Meow," Azrael said, clearly meaning "You dumb bird."

The Smurfs quickly crossed the rickety old wooden bridge leading from the wizard's home.

Smurfette glanced over her shoulder. "Azrael's gaining on us!"

Monty had freed himself and was overhead as well. The bird took a nosedive at the bridge.

"Incoming bird!" Clumsy warned the others.

Monty crashed hard. He hit the bridge at such a high speed, it split the wooden planks in two. The Smurfs were holding on to one end. Azrael was hanging from the other.

"This might hurt!" Hefty warned as the bridge swung like a rope toward the rocky cliffs ahead.

"WWAAAAAAAHHHH!!!!!" Clumsy's scream went on and on.

The Smurfs slammed into the mountainside.

"OOF!" Clumsy lost his grip and fell. His scream continued. "AHHHHHHHHHHH!"

Team Smurf all looked nervously down, only to discover they were only a few inches off the ground. Clumsy wasn't falling at all. He was lying flat on a rock below them—still screaming in panic.

Brainy, Smurfette, and Hefty hopped down and helped Clumsy up. Then they scampered away.

"Come on! Smurf this way!" Hefty took the lead.

At the top of the cliff, on the other side of the ravine, Azrael climbed to the edge of the cliffside, where he watched them get away.

Azrael called to Monty and pointed in the Smurfs' direction. "MEOW!! MEOW!"

Monty took off and soared over the Smurfs, but they ducked into an opening in the rocks to hide.

"Dohhohohohohoho!" Monty shrieked.

"RUN FASTER!! RUN FASTER!" Smurfette yelled.

"WHY ARE OUR LEGS SO SHORT?!" Brainy complained.

"WHY ARE OUR FEET SO BIG?!" Clumsy said as he tripped for the millionth time.

"WHY ARE MY MUSCLES SO BIG?" shouted Hefty.

"REALLY, MAN?" Brainy yelled.

"Dohhohohohohoho!" Monty hooted as he dove at them again.

At last, they reached the old hollowed-out log entrance to Smurf Village. Hefty, Brainy, and Smurfette dashed inside, but Clumsy tripped and was left outside the hidden entry, hanging from the edge of the log. Monty was headed straight for him.

"Um, guys! A little help here?" Clumsy's voice was tight with fear.

Monty was getting closer and closer!

He called louder, "He's coming! He's coming!"

Hefty dashed back and grabbed Clumsy, hoisting him over his shoulder and then running to safety. The log teeter-tottered over just as Monty overshot the distance and toppled right into a rock.

"Dohhohohohohoho." Monty shook off the fall and scanned the whole area. He was confused—Where'd they go?

The Smurfs were so happy to be home. They cheered and high-fived and hugged one another saying, "Woo-hoo!" and "Yeah!" and "All right!"

They'd have gone on celebrating all day, but then they noticed Papa Smurf was standing there, glaring at them, arms crossed over his chest. "Well, I know four Smurfs who have some explaining to do," he said.

Their cheers turned into worries. "Oh boy," Hefty muttered.

"That's not good," added Brainy.

Clumsy smiled meekly. "Hi."

36

# Chapter 5

The members of Team Smurf were speaking all at once, trying to explain to Papa what had happened.

It sounded like a jumble of words, and it was impossible to tell who was saying what:

"Oh my gosh, Papa, you won't believe it!"

"Smurfboarding!"

"Out of nowhere—mystery Smurf!"

"He lost his hat!"

"Ran into the Forbidden Forest!"

"Could be another village!"

"A giant vulture swooped down!"

"Locked in a cage!"

"Gargamel had Freeze Balls!"

"He had a map!"

"Gargamel is going to get them!"

"We have to go to the Forbidden Forest!"

"Three Tall Trees!"

"We got there just in time!"

"Hefty saved us all!"

"Hefty shot us out on a crossbow!"

The way they were telling it, Papa Smurf couldn't understand the whole story. "One at a time—one at a time! Please! Please!" Finally, he whistled loudly to get them to stop. It worked.

From the bits he gathered, he said, "I've told you time and again, the Forbidden Forest is forbidden!" He shook his head. "And now you're talking about maps and mystery Smurfs and Gargamel's lair!"

Hefty looked like he had something to say, but Papa wasn't about to let them start explaining again. He went on. "None of what you're saying makes any sense! And I really don't understand why you can't follow simple rules. You snuck out, and it put you all in danger! Seems to me the only way I can keep you safe is if you're grounded!"

Hefty, Clumsy, and Brainy immediately started complaining:

"Grounded?!"

"WHAT?!"

"That's not fair!"

"But, Papa!"

"Come on!"

Papa Smurf wouldn't listen to their excuses. This was serious. "No buts! None of you are to take one step out of your mushrooms without telling me where you're going. Do you understand that?"

Smurfette knew Papa was serious. There was no way they'd convince him to let them go after Gargamel. Better to take the punishment and then find a way out of it.

"You're right, Papa," Smurfette said.

Papa didn't believe his blue ears! "Huh? What?"

"HUH? What?" Brainy and the others echoed.

Smurfette glared at the boys. "You're right. I don't know *what* we were thinking."

Papa gave her a long look, then said, "Uh . . . good. Because as I was saying . . . you all behaved completely irresponsibly!"

"Yes! Right! Exactly! Couldn't agree more. Right, guys?!" Smurfette was taking charge. There was no time to waste.

The boys were baffled. They started talking at the same time again:

"Right?"

"Excuse me?"

"Uh, what are you talking about, Smurfette?"

Papa regained his composure. "Yes, so, and furthermore—"

Papa was preparing to continue his lecture about their irresponsible behavior, but Smurfette cut in. "In fact, I think we should all go to our rooms right now and think about what we've done."

"Well, I think that's—"

"Tough but fair," Smurfette finished. She started to usher her friends out the door, pushing and pulling to prod them along. "C'mon, guys."

"What's your endgame here, Smurfette?" Brainy asked.

"Okay, okay, I'm moving." Clumsy stumbled forward.

"Did you get pecked on the noggin?" Hefty wanted to know.

"Actually, Smurfette—" Papa had more to say.

Smurfette opened the door and gave the boys a shove outside. Looking back over her shoulder, she said, "Don't worry, Papa. We are certainly going to do some thinking about what we did. And so forth. And we will definitely not be leaving our rooms until we have thought this whole thing out. And then, for good measure, we'll think about it some more."

"Yes, but . . ." Papa Smurf rubbed his beard.

"Great talk, Papa." She was the last to leave, and closed the door behind her.

Papa stood there for a beat, totally confused by what just happened, and then went back to his chair, saying, "I have no idea what I'm doing."

Smurfette felt bad about lying to Papa, but she knew in her heart that the other Smurf Village needed her help. When she got back to her mushroom, she filled her backpack with the essentials: water canteen, blanket, a firefly flashlight, some snacks, and her hairbrush.

On the way out, she peeked in the mirror. That mirror reflected another mirror, which reflected itself, creating the image of infinite Smurfettes. With a confident nod, Smurfette snuck out.

Smurfette hurried to put distance between herself and Smurf Village. High above the hidden valley, she turned to look back one last time. There was no going home until she found the other village and warned its inhabitants about Gargamel.

Feeling a bit nervous about her mission, she walked on until she reached a large stone wall, near where she'd discovered the strange Smurf hat. She quickly found the tiny opening that she'd seen the other Smurf go through. With a deep breath, she began to enter, when suddenly Smurfette heard something rustling in the bushes. She stopped in her tracks, filled with fear, but then she realized what—or who—had made the noise.

"Hefty," Smurfette said. "I know that's you."

He stepped out.

"'Sup, Smurfette," he said, just as more rustling came from the bushes behind him.

"Brainy?" Smurfette said before she saw him.

"How'd you do that?" he asked.

She smiled. "And I assume Clumsy . . ."

With a whoosh and a thud, Clumsy fell from a high tree, landing near Hefty.

"What are you guys doing out here?" Smurfette asked as Clumsy dusted himself off.

"We knew you were up to something," Hefty told her.

"This is all my fault, Hefty," she explained.

"But, Smurfette, the Forbidden Forest?" Hefty

moved into her path, blocking the way. "It's too dangerous."

She knew he was right. "I have to at least warn that lost village."

"Well, we're Team Smurf, and we stick together so . . ." Hefty moved aside and stood next to her. "We're going with you."

"I can't ask you to do that," she protested.

"You didn't ask. We volunteered," Hefty replied.

"We volunteered," Clumsy agreed.

Smurfette quickly understood this was one fight she'd never win. Her friends would have her back no matter what. "Thanks, guys."

"First things first," Brainy said. He placed Snappy Bug down on a sheet of paper, and all the Smurfs gathered 'round as she drew them a map. It was just like the map they'd seen in Gargamel's lair, featuring three tall trees!

Clumsy was impressed. "Wow. Bug technology. Cool."

Brainy studied the drawing. "According to my map, we should be . . ." He glanced around. "Standing right in front of this very large, tall stone wall."

They looked around and saw the stone wall looming over them.

"Check!" Brainy said.

Hefty was going to take the lead, going first through the hole in the wall, but Smurfette stopped him. She took a deep breath and went in, her friends following close behind. . . .

# Chapter 6

The Forbidden Forest was uncharted territory for the Smurfs in Smurf Village, so as Brainy saw it, they were conducting groundbreaking research! He didn't want to miss a thing, so he immediately began to record his thoughts with the help of Snappy Bug.

"One small step for four small Smurfs," he said proudly . . . before stepping right into a spiderweb. "Ahhhh! Yuck!"

Smurfette couldn't believe her eyes. Everything was bright and colorful and smurftastic! "Wow, wow, wow, wow, wow . . . WOW!" she gasped. She ran from rock to bush to plant, checking it all out. "AHHHH!"

Smurfette was gobbled up by a large flower.

Hefty rushed over, shouting, "Smurfette! You okay, Smurfette?"

Both Hefty and Brainy got close enough to also be gobbled up.

Clumsy was alone. Very slowly, he approached the flower. "Nice flowers . . . Nice flowers . . ."

All the flowers nearby started bending toward him, surrounding him. "NOT NICE FLOWERS!!!" he shrieked. Quickly turning, Clumsy tried to bolt away, but he ran right into the open mouth of a flower he hadn't noticed.

Team Smurf was chewed up, spit out, and then gobbled up again, as the flowers each checked them out by tasting them.

"Ahhhhh! Ahhhhhhhh! Ahhhhhh!" Brainy screamed every time his flower opened its mouth.

Then all at once, the flowers decided they didn't like the flavor of Smurf and spit them out one by one, hurling them deep into the Forbidden Forest.

Smurfette, Hefty, and Brainy each landed with a thud, covered in gooey, slimy plant saliva, but still in one piece.

Smurfette looked around. "Where's Clumsy?"

A second later, Clumsy shot out of the carnivorous flower and landed face-first into a Kissing Plant, which showered him with juicy red-lipstick kisses. He tried to wrestle away, but the Kissing Plant hugged him tightly with its vines.

"Hey—we just met! I'm not that kind of Smurf!" Clumsy broke free, wiping the lipstick marks off his face. He plucked a leaf from a nearby plant to finish cleaning his face. Of course, this was a Boxing Plant, which started throwing punches like nobody's business. Clumsy took a direct hit to the nose and fell backward, rolling down a hill.

"Watch out for the steep embankment!" Brainy said, a second too late.

When the rest of Team Smurf found Clumsy, he was lying in the soft grass, eyes closed.

"Clumsy? You okay?" Smurfette asked.

He opened his eyes and stared past her at some tiny glowing lights far above. "I'm seeing stars," he said.

Floating all around them were giant iridescent winged insects.

"Wowwww!" the Smurfs all exclaimed together. The bugs filled the sky.

One of them swooped down.

"It looks friendly." Clumsy reached out toward the biggest one. In baby talk he asked, "What's your name?"

The big bug sniffed Clumsy's hat, then let out a sneeze, followed by a burst of fire from its mouth. The tip of Clumsy's hat turned black from smoldering flames.

The other Smurfs moved in for a closer look.

Brainy was thrilled. He flipped through a book. "Amazing—a winged, fire-breathing anisoptera. Let's see . . . how should we classify this?"

Snappy Bug helped, making suggestions in cute little squeaking noises.

"Hmmm, maybe. It seems like an easy choice," he replied. "But I'm just not sure."

"How about Dragon . . . fly?" Smurfette suggested, because of the way it breathed fire.

"Yeah. Okay. Let's go with Dragonfly," Brainy concluded.

Clumsy stepped carefully away from the big bug. "Hopefully, it's more *fly* than dragon."

Suddenly, the Dragonfly grabbed Clumsy by the head and carried him off!

"Nope! Less fly! LESS FLYYYYYYYY!" he screamed when he saw that he was being taken to the Dragonfly's nest.

His friends laughed, but Clumsy didn't find it funny at all.

"Uhhh, guys!" The Dragonfly dropped Clumsy into the nest with her other eggs and then sat down on him to keep him warm. "I'm okay! A little help here?" Clumsy called to his friends.

Down below, Gargamel, Azrael, and Monty made their way through the opening into the Forbidden Forest. They were also swept up into the flowers' mouths and spit out the same way.

"AHHHHH!! OOF! Ohhh." Gargamel swatted at his bird, who landed on top of him.

"Dohhohohohohoho," Monty replied.

"Monty, get off of me!" the wizard shouted. They were all covered in goopy flower nectar. "Argh! I hate nature! Oh gawdy!"

One of the Smurf-tasting plants hissed and snapped Gargamel's nose.

"AHHHH!!!! Azrael, do something! Stop laughing! This is *not* funny!"

Another plant grabbed the wizard's ankles.

Gargamel was furious. "Grrrr, wretched Forbidden Forest . . ." This was not going well.

Azrael sat safely to the side, purring and laughing. But then the Kissing Plants found him, covering the cat in lipstick kisses.

Monty couldn't help because he was having his own issues with some sort of odd eyeball plants.

"Let—me—go!" Gargamel told the flowers. They did, spitting him out with a heavy thunk onto the forest floor.

Team Smurf looked up to the sky, where high above them, a moving canopy of hundreds of Dragonflies flew through the air. The sun reflected through their iridescent wings. In the trees hung hundreds of nests.

"These nests are made of some material I've never seen before," Brainy said, looking around.

"WHOA! OOF!" Clumsy managed to escape the Dragonfly nest to join the group. "You know, I think I've had enough of these flying antipastos for one day."

Suddenly, a shadow passed above, one that clearly wasn't a Dragonfly.

It was Monty, and he was blocking their path!

The Smurfs turned to run, but Azrael was in the way, licking his lips with a fearsome "Meow!"

And finally, from behind a boulder stepped a sinister, smiling Gargamel.

"Hey! What are you doing here?" Clumsy asked, a little baffled by the wizard's presence.

"I was thinking of getting a place out here, just a quiet place in the forest. It's a little breezy on the hill. . . . What do you think I'm doing out here, idiot?" Gargamel growled sarcastically.

"You are never going to find that village, Gargamel!" Smurfette said.

Gargamel laughed at her. "Oh, Smurfette! If it weren't for you, I wouldn't even have known about those other Smurfs. Get 'em, boys!"

At that, Monty and Azrael charged toward the Smurfs.

"Smurfentine formation, go!" Hefty shouted, and the Smurfs scattered.

Azrael and Monty smashed into each other.

Clumsy ran around Gargamel's feet screaming "Smurfentine," which confused the wizard long enough for Hefty to smack Gargamel in the shins with a branch.

"AHHHH!" the wizard shrieked.

Brainy dodged Azrael. "Smurfentine!"

"Smurfentine!" Smurfette shouted as she ran in the other direction.

51

Gargamel was spinning. Smurfs were attacking him from all angles. He tipped his head back and accidentally knocked an egg out of one of the Dragonfly nests. Before it could fall too far, he caught it. The Dragonflies above were angry and agitated, giving Gargamel an evil idea.

He looked at Clumsy. "Hey, you! You're the clumsy one, right?"

Clumsy stopped running. "Huh?"

"Think fast!" Gargamel tossed the egg into Clumsy's arms.

"I caught it!" Clumsy looked at the egg and then at the angry Dragonflies. "This isn't good. . . ."

The Dragonflies were now all focused on Clumsy! They swarmed around him and the other Smurfs.

"Clumsy! Give 'em back their egg!" Hefty ordered.

"Okay," Clumsy replied. He wanted to get rid of the egg, but no matter what he did, it ended up back in his hands. "Oh, come on," he muttered as the situation got more and more desperate.

"Clumsy!" Hefty shouted.

"I'm trying," Clumsy said as a Dragonfly flame nipped at his butt. "YEOOOWWW!"

"Over there!" Smurfette shouted, seeing some rabbit holes up ahead that they could hide in. They all made a mad dash for safety.

Smurfette jumped into one of the holes in the ground. The rest of Team Smurf was right behind her.

"I'm sorry I poached your egg!" Clumsy set the egg on the ground as he leaped into the nearest hole. A Dragonfly swooped in and grabbed the egg, and then, working together, the Dragonflies blew fire into the rabbit holes.

Gargamel, Azrael, and Monty laughed with joy.

"Ha-ha! Well, they're dead." Gargamel rubbed his hands together gleefully.

"Meow, meow." Azrael wasn't so sure. "Meow!"

Gargamel argued, saying, "Ahh, it doesn't matter. What are a few worthless pennies when there's a pot of gold at the end of my rainbow?"

"Meow," Azrael countered, making his point.

"Oh, Azrael, I haven't had this much fun since we renovated the hovel."

"Meow."

"Can it, fuzzball! They're dead!" the wizard replied firmly.

"Meow, meow, meow," Azrael continued arguing as they began heading back toward the path.

"DEAD, I say!" Gargamel insisted.

"Meow, meow, meow." Azrael tried to get the last word, but the wizard ignored him.

# Chapter 7

Inside the rabbit warren, Team Smurf was still in one piece— Well, each Smurf was in one piece, anyway. The gang had been split up, with each Smurf pushed into a different cavernous, tubelike passageway. They were all alone, desperately searching for the others.

Brainy felt around in the dark for an exit.

"Hello?" Smurfette called.

"Smurfette?!" Hefty answered her.

"Echo! Echo! Echo!" Clumsy called out into the darkness. "I, uh—don't do well in the darkness," he said, his voice trembling. "I have enough trouble in the daylight!"

Brainy took charge, shouting through the tunnels. "Hold on, everyone. We need to find a way out of here."

"Wow! That is good thinking, 'Brainy.'" Hefty snorted. *Obviously* they needed to find a way out, but first they needed to find one another.

"Guys . . . ?" Smurfette called to the others.

"Darkness!" Clumsy said, a bit more panicked this time. Where was everyone?!

Hefty tried to calm him down. "Don't be scared; just think happy thoughts."

"It's not really happy times right now," Clumsy countered.

"Just stay in the light, Clumsy," Smurfette suggested.

There were some small rays of light coming from breaks in the ground. He could see them up ahead.

"Too late." Clumsy was too scared to calm down. "I'm walking into the darkness."

"What? Why are you— Why?" Hefty just wanted them all to stay still.

"I'm really freaking out, you guys!" Clumsy snapped back.

"Stop!" Brainy called out before Clumsy could go too far. Brainy had prepared for this. "Everyone go into your backpacks, get out your Emergency

Tunnel Survival Kit. Find the small glass vial marked 'light' and shake it."

Clumsy found a jar in his pack. He shook the jar gently, and a firefly inside lit up. Now he could see the path through the lonely tunnel.

Brainy checked in on his nervous friend, shouting, "Clumsy? How you doin'?"

"Uhhh. Okay, I guess," Clumsy said, staring at the firefly light as he searched through the pack to see what else Brainy had packed.

"Just hang tight, Clumsy. I'm not sure how long this'll take or how long we'll be down here. So, everybody, whatever you do, don't eat all your rations!" Brainy really had thought of everything.

"I just ate all my rations!" Clumsy cried, dropping the wrappers to the ground.

"Clumsy!" Hefty said, rolling his eyes.

"I'm stress eating!" Clumsy was out of control.

Smurfette shouted, "I'm coming, Clumsy! Follow the sound of my voice—"

"Wait!" Brainy cut in, trying to stop her. "These tunnels are like a maze; we'll just get more lost."

"We gotta do something!" Smurfette said back.

"I'm with her—time for some action!" Hefty

was ready to head out on his own.

"We're doing this all wrong," Brainy said. But he didn't have a better idea—yet.

"Smurfette?!?" Clumsy called her name into the dark.

"I'm close Clumsy, almost there!" Smurfette told him.

"That's just the echo playing tricks on us," Brainy warned.

Clumsy continued to panic. "Anybody?!"

"I'm here, I'm here, right around this corner." Smurfette turned down another tunnel.

"Hey, everybody! My light is going out." Clumsy's voice was shaking.

Smurfette continued down the way she thought she heard him. "Clumsy?!" Her voice echoed.

Hefty heard the distress in Smurfette's voice. "That's it, I'm punching us outta here!" He began violently pummeling the wall with his fists. "Hwah! HWAH! HWAH-HWAH-HWAH!"

The ceiling above Smurfette began to crumble. "It's collapsing!"

"Hefty! Put those fists away before you get us killed!" Brainy shrieked.

"At least I'm trying something!" Hefty took another hit at the wall.

"I'm gonna blow us outta here," Clumsy said. He'd found an exploding energy drink in his pack.

Brainy shouted, "No!"

"Yeah!" Hefty loved the idea.

"Don't!" Smurfette said.

"Too late!" Clumsy tossed the energy drink into the tunnel wall and *KABOOM*!

"Clum . . . sy?" Smurfette found him. Finally, they were together.

But the celebration was short-lived. Beady eyes filled the dark tunnel, every one of them fixed on the four Smurfs. Suddenly, the ground began to rumble, and out of the darkness, a stampede of green bunnies flooded the caves.

Smurfette began to run, then jumped up onto a bunny, as if it was an oversize horse. "Wahhhhhahahahahahahhaaaaa!"

"Hey, Smurfette!" She looked over to see Clumsy riding a bunny too.

Smurfette followed him through the warren.

Brainy and Hefty each captured their own rabbits. When Hefty passed Clumsy, he grabbed him so they rode together on his rabbit. "Whoa! Ha-ha! Hang on, Clumsy bro! I got you, little buddy."

Riding "bunnyback," the Smurfs burst out of the underground labyrinth.

The frenzied herd of bunnies charged out after them, swarming from the tunnels and into the forest.

"STAMPEEEEEDE!" Brainy shrieked.

Clumsy, still riding with Hefty, was feeling a little ill. "I think my rations are coming up!"

Next to them, Smurfette was looking like a pro. Her bunny reared up on its hind legs and released a sort of rabbit-horse sound. Then it sped up, lunging forward and skillfully banking off trees along the way and sailing farther ahead.

Hefty and Clumsy weren't having such an easy time. They quickly got bucked off their bunny and landed on the back of Smurfette's. Brainy landed on hers too, but he was facedown, backside up. His glasses came to rest on his tail, making his butt look like a face.

"What?!" Brainy asked, not understanding why everyone was laughing. "What's so funny?!"

"Now that's what I call 'talking out of your

60

© Peyo

© Peyo

© Peyo

butt.'" Hefty laughed so hard he was tearing up.

As Brainy tried to regain his dignity, Smurfette noticed something in the distance. "Oh, boooyyyys!" She pointed with joy. "Would anyone be interested in knowing that we are in sight of the Three Tall Trees?"

"Woo-hoo!" they cheered.

Smurfette patted her bunny on the back of his neck. "And Bucky is going to get us there extra fast!"

"Bucky?" Clumsy asked.

"Seems like a Bucky to me. Look at his teeth!" She gave him a little kick like he was a horse. "Hit it, Bucky!" She giggled as Bucky zoomed them closer to their goal.

Meanwhile, back in Smurf Village, Papa went to visit Smurfette at her mushroom. He knocked, but there was no answer from inside.

He spoke through the door. "Smurfette? Before you say anything, just listen. Now, I know yesterday I might've been a bit tough on you and the boys. And I know there are times I'm a little overprotective."

There was no response from inside, so he went on.

"Okay, a *lot* overprotective. But you have to understand—you snuck out. You have to be more careful!" He was upset, but he stopped for a long moment to collect himself. "Smurfette, I know lately you may not realize it, and I may not say it enough, but you are—You shine. So, anyway, we're smurfy? I think you and your brothers have been grounded long enough." He expected her to come out, happy to hear that her punishment was over.

Instead, there was no reply.

"Smurfette?" Papa asked again. "Okay, I'm opening the door, and I'm walking in to talk more. You there? Smurfette?" He twisted the doorknob and slowly entered Smurfette's mushroom. It was immediately obvious she wasn't there. He was at first shocked, and then he became suspicious.

Papa went to Hefty's mushroom. "Hefty!" He rushed to Hefty's bed—it looked like Hefty was in it. But Papa pulled back the covers to find it was just a barbell.

"Brainy!" At Brainy's house, it looked like Brainy was standing at his blackboard, but actually, it was a dummy made up of objects from Brainy's lab.

Papa was getting very angry as he went to Clumsy's mushroom. "CLUMSY!" He pulled back Clumsy's bedcovers and found three apples there. "Oh, that's not even convincing!" Papa said. The apples didn't look like a Smurf at all.

Papa Smurf marched out of the mushroom and then announced, "When I find those Smurfs, I will ground them for a month of blue moons!"

Just then, Nosey strolled by the window. "Hmm, what's going on in here?" Papa slammed the window shut. "Hmm, well, all right."

# Chapter 8

Team Smurf rode the giant bunny, Bucky, together through the dense woods and vast valleys, in the direction of the Three Tall Trees. Day faded to night, when the moonlight cascaded through the treetops. The darker it got, the more Bucky began to glow like a giant bunny flashlight.

"Wow!" Smurfette exclaimed, looking around from the bunny into the forest, which was illuminated as well. "Have you ever seen something so beautiful?"

Hefty turned to face Smurfette, full of sincerity. "Every day, Smurfette. Every. Day."

"Don't be weird," Brainy chided, rolling his eyes.

"You don't be weird," Hefty said crossly in return.

It was very late when Bucky started to slow down, clearly hungry and sniffing for food.

Clumsy was mumbling in his sleep as they rode. Brainy let out a yawn.

"We can camp here for the night," Brainy said, gesturing to a clearing. They all rolled off Bucky and started stretching. "I'll start us a fire. Fetch me some firewood, would ya, Hefty?"

"Um, a 'please' would be nice," Hefty grumbled.

"Yes, it would, but I haven't earned my manners badge, so get me some firewood." Brainy pointed to a thick stand of trees.

Hefty muttered to himself as he collected sticks, while Brainy referred to the campfire-building chapter of his book.

"Clumsy, you okay?" Smurfette asked, sitting down beside him.

"Yeah, sure . . . ," Clumsy said, reflecting on the day. "It's been fun. Well, not *tons* of fun, but it had its moments. Kind of. You know what I'm trying to say." He finally sighed and admitted, "It hasn't been that much fun."

Hefty dropped a load of wood in front of Brainy.

"Well done, Hefty, well done," Brainy said. Then

referring to the instructions in the chapter, he said, "All right. Step one: The wood should be stacked in a tepee-like structure." He stacked it. "Step two: I tap this flint with a rock and . . ." Brainy tried, but nothing happened. A few small sparks sputtered into smoke. He tried blowing on the wood to ignite a spark, but still nothing.

"You're not even blowing on it; you're spitting on it," Hefty said.

"Hmmm, that's odd. Perhaps the wood you collected was damp, Hefty. According to my manual, it should spark right up." Brainy read the page again.

"Hey, I've got an idea." Hefty grabbed the manual and threw it onto the pile of wood and *WHOOOOSH!* The sticks instantly erupted into a huge bonfire that lit the surrounding area.

"No, no, no, no, no, no!" Brainy quickly reached into the fire and pulled out his smoking book, flustered.

"You know, you're right, Brain Man. . . . Your little book *does* come in handy," Hefty said, smiling.

Brainy was furious. "Shame . . . shame on you. We'd be lost without this book."

Hefty started talking in a hoity-toity voice,

imitating Brainy. "My name is Brainy. I'm the supersmart Smurf."

Smurfette laughed at Brainy and Hefty as she brushed Bucky's fur. They were acting like brothers, fighting and arguing over the silliest things.

Brainy checked his manual. "Okay, the damage is minimal, and the binding is still intact." He took a whiff. "Smells good."

The Smurfs settled in around the campfire, gazing up at the night sky. Bucky was having a dinner of carrots and grass.

"Just think, guys," Smurfette said, tucking her hands behind her head. "After all this time, while we've been going about our smurfy business back home, there've been other Smurfs out there, just like us."

"Or they could be *nothing* like us," Brainy said.

"He's right. We should be prepared for whatever we find," Hefty said. "Those other Smurfs might not even be blue."

"Maybe they'll be orange," Clumsy said. "I like orange."

"What if they all wear glasses?" Brainy dreamed.

"Or have big, bushy mustaches?"

"What if they have scaly skin and sharp teeth?" Brainy shuddered at the thought.

"And giant claws and little beady eyes," Hefty added, causing Brainy to shiver even more.

Smurfette didn't buy it; she was still convinced the new Smurfs would be as great as her own friends.

Clumsy tried to make a shadow puppet in the firelight. But of course, Clumsy was terrible at shadow puppets, so he just flashed both hands in shadow up on the trunk of a tree. "What if they have . . . HANDS!"

Team Smurf roared with laughter this time.

"Listen, they could be very different from us, but I was different. Papa found the goodness inside me," Smurfette told the others. "These Smurfs deserve the same chance I was given. I need to do this."

"And we're gonna help you. We're Team Smurf, and we're in this together." Hefty gave her an awkwardly long smile. "And by 'together' I mean 'me and you.' And those guys. But mostly me and you." He was flirting again.

Brainy moved around the others, holding out his Snappy Bug on a selfie-stick made from a regular stick. "Okay, everyone: smurfy selfie time!"

Snappy played a recording that said, "Say 'blue cheese!'"

"Blue cheese!" they said together.

The photo showed all of them happy and smiling, but Clumsy had his eyes closed.

Before sunrise, they started moving again. The four Smurfs rode on Bucky's back, more comfortably now that they'd had some rest. Bucky leaped over a hill and then skidded to screeching halt!

The Smurfs climbed down to see what had surprised the bunny. "According to this, we should be arriving at a river," Brainy announced, his face still buried in the map.

"Check," the other Smurfs said. It was a river, but not just any river. The flow surged and swelled, undulating in an almost-hypnotic state. The water was so clear they could see schools of glowing fish and bioluminescent sparkles. It was enchanting.

Hefty blinked hard. "It's like a workout for my eyeballs."

They climbed onto Bucky's back, and Smurfette said, "Okay, Bucky. Let's see how fast you can swim. Hiiya!"

The bunny refused to move.

"C'mon, boy. You can do it," Smurfette encouraged him.

Nope. Bucky backed away from the river, shaking his head in fear.

"What's a little water?" Hefty didn't understand the bunny's reaction.

"What's that, Bucky?" Clumsy acted as if he understood bunny-language. "The river is unsafe and full of dangerous surprises at every bend?" Clumsy was pretty sure that's what the bunny meant.

Brainy didn't think that was right. "No, I didn't get any of that. Perhaps Glow-Bunnies just don't swim."

Hefty looked around, analyzing the situation. "That's too bad. We'd get there so much faster."

Brainy had a brilliant idea. "Aha! Fear not, my intrepid Team Smurf." He pointed at another badge on his backpack. "I didn't earn this raft building merit badge for nothing!"

Brainy consulted his manual.

Snappy Bug drew up the plans.

Brainy started building. He sawed wood and pounded nails until he fist-bumped himself and said, "Boom! Nailed it!" The raft was finished, and it looked amazing!

"Impressive, Brainy!" Smurfette exclaimed.

They all started to pile on when Hefty stopped Clumsy. "Here." He grabbed a doughnut-shaped flower blossom from a nearby plant and placed it over Clumsy's head like a life jacket.

"Oooh, stylish and practical," Clumsy said as he admired it.

Now they were ready.

They each said their good-byes to Bucky and prepared to push the raft into the water.

"Let's launch this bad boy!" Hefty exclaimed, ready to get moving.

"Wait! Remember, this strange river may hold untold surprises," Brainy warned. "We must be cautious!"

"Cautious. Good point. And heave . . . ," Hefty started again.

But Brainy was still wary. "Wait! Currents can be unpredictable. We must be alert and vigilant."

"Vigilance. Good call. On three, two—"

"Wait!" Brainy cut in again. "We must make sure we always—"

"Beep, blop, blorp." Hefty talked over him in annoying sounds.

"Pay attention to the—"

"Bong, bong, bing, bang!" Hefty went on.

"Rate of speed of the—"

"Beep, bop, bingo, bango, bing, bing, bang, bop." Brainy gave up.

"Okay." Hefty smiled, knowing he'd won. "And we're off! HEEEEAAVE-HO!"

They pushed the raft off the bank and into the river and then settled down for the ride.

Smurfette waved at Bucky, who was watching them nervously from the shore. "Don't worry; we'll be fine!"

The entire team waved and called out, "Bye, Bucky! Thank you! We'll see you on the way back!"

Bucky nodded and waved his paw.

As the raft gained speed, Clumsy noticed a lever that read "Emergency." "Hey. What's this thing?"

"I wouldn't touch that if I were you," Brainy told him.

Clumsy sat on his hands, complaining, "Oh, now all I want to do is touch it."

"At this pace Gargamel doesn't stand a chance!"

Smurfette said as they barreled down the river.

The early morning sunlight created a calming, beautiful atmosphere, and yet, it was also too quiet and a little eerie.

Smurfette pointed at the map and said, "Look! If we follow this river, we'll be right on course—"

"Right on course to the end of our rainbow," Gargamel finished Smurfette's sentence, then laughed.

# Chapter 9

"Gargamel!" Smurfette exclaimed the instant she saw the evil wizard.

Gargamel and his crew had made their own raft out of a floating log. Azrael was using Monty like an outboard motor, the bird's tail dipped in the water for propulsion.

"Smurfs!" Gargamel couldn't believe his eyes. "I thought I left you for dead!"

Clumsy pinched his lips together and stared at the emergency lever on the raft. This certainly seemed like an emergency to him. . . .

"Gun it!" Gargamel ordered Monty.

"Hang on, Smurf crew!" Hefty told the others. The raft began to move faster in the water. They pulled ahead of Gargamel's log.

"What the— NO!" The evil wizard grabbed

a stick from the riverbank. He shouted at Team Smurf, "Stop ruining everything. I'm the one who ruins things!" Then he began to paddle his log toward the Smurfs, trying to knock them over into the swirling river.

Hefty slammed his fist into Gargamel's stick until the weapon was nothing more than a nub in the wizard's hand.

"What? Azrael, get me a bigger stick." He tossed the tiny piece of wood aside, then looked up. His eyes went wide with fear!

Team Smurf also panicked when they noticed what was right in front of them all.

It was Enchanted Rapids! A crazy, treacherous, and magical roller coaster ride of swirling water with bumps and spins.

"Oh dear," Gargamel gasped. Azrael meowed nervously as they got closer and closer.

"Clumsy! Pull the lever!" Brainy shouted.

"Seriously?! But you said not to! Is this a trick?"

"PULL IT NOW!" Brainy and Smurfette ordered at the same time.

Clumsy tugged at the emergency lever. A sailing mast immediately popped up.

The rapids sent Gargamel and his log flying into the air and underwater.

"WHAAAAAAAAAAAA!" Gargamel shrieked.

Harnessing the wind into the raft's sail, Hefty easily steered them a safe distance away. But when they hit another rapid, Clumsy was thrown overboard. "Whoa!" He landed on Gargamel's log, running in place to keep from falling over.

Gargamel kept churning through the swiftly moving water, cursing as his head popped up and down. "What the—? Son—of—a— This—stupid—— Really—ticks—me—off! This—river—is—killing—me!"

Azrael lunged for Clumsy, but was knocked back by a huge wave, just as Clumsy was thrown safely back onto the Smurfs' raft. Team Smurf was fully engulfed in the rapids at this point, but they were working together to navigate.

"Look out!" Brainy called as he noticed a huge boulder coming their way.

Team Smurf ducked in time, but Gargamel didn't. The wizard and his pets saw the rock just before it hit them.

"Meow," Azrael muttered.

"I love you, too," Gargamel said to his cat, just before a wave hit and they were both sucked under.

"Yeah! We did it!" the Smurfs shouted.

"Sink or swim!"

"Gargamel's toast!"

"Take that!"

Then, from behind, they heard a cry for help. It was Gargamel, struggling to stay afloat.

Brainy ignored him, saying, "All right! We're still on course!" In the distance, they could see the Three Tall Trees.

"Double-time it, Hefty!" Smurfette was excited they were so close, but with one last look behind them, she saw Gargamel still battling the rapids.

"Help! I'm sinking! Please! I'm afraid of turtles!" Gargamel thrashed his arms.

"Um, guys, what's he up to now?" Clumsy asked the others.

Brainy wanted to keep moving. "Forget that guy!"

Gargamel begged them. "HELP! My cat can't swim!"

Suddenly, everyone on the raft got very quiet. All the Smurfs were staring at Gargamel, deciding what to do. Hefty was the first to speak up. "We gotta help him."

"Are you crazy? Why?!" Brainy demanded.

"Because it's what I do," Hefty said simply.

"Listen to him!" Gargamel said between gulps of air.

"But he's our sworn enemy!" Brainy reminded Hefty.

"He's *literally* a villain!" Clumsy added.

"I can change!" The wizard was splashing in the river a little more frantically now.

"And I *literally* wear my heart on my sleeve, okay?" Hefty turned to show them his heart tattoo.

"That's your shoulder. Not a sleeve," Brainy pointed out, rolling his eyes.

"I like your tattoo!" Gargamel called back.

Hefty couldn't let the wizard drown. "We're doing this." He began to turn the raft.

"Smurfette, talk some sense into him!" Brainy pleaded with her.

Hefty glanced at Smurfette, who was debating the problem. "Brainy, I hate Gargamel more than anyone, but we're Smurfs. We do the right thing."

"Thank goodness for it," Gargamel said.

"We have to save him," Smurfette told the others.

"I just want to go on record that I'm decisively against this," Brainy said.

"Whatever, we're doing it." Hefty moved the boat closer to the wizard.

"Sounds awesome." Gargamel was anxious to be rescued.

Smurfette grabbed the doughnut-shaped blossom life vest from Clumsy and handed it to Hefty. "Here, use this!"

Hefty steered the raft into position and threw the flower. "Grab on!"

"I don't know about this." Brainy was worried.

Gargamel pulled himself up. "You won't regret it. Thank you, thank you, such a kind Smurf."

"Are you okay?" Hefty asked.

"I'm okay. Wet, tired, kind of waterlogged. Thanks for asking, but I'm still evil so . . ." With a swipe of his hand, he knocked the Smurfs into the water and claimed their raft for himself. "Enjoy drowning!" He laughed. "Hope you're better swimmers than you are judges of a wizard's character!"

Monty and Azrael made themselves comfortable on the raft.

The Smurfs were separated in the churning waters. They floated for a few moments in the wild rapids, and then ... they disappeared over the edge of a cliff and down a massive waterfall.

"AHHHHHHHHHHHHHH!"

Smurfette, Hefty, Brainy, and Clumsy all disappeared into the mist.

# Chapter 10

Smurfette was washed ashore in a blue lagoon. She landed facedown in the sand. Scattered nearby on the shore were Hefty and Brainy.

Smurfette sputtered and coughed. "Brainy?! Hefty?! You okay?"

Brainy choked out, "Define 'okay.'"

Smurfette looked around for Clumsy. "Where's Clumsy?" she asked the others,

Hefty got up, brushed off the sand, and started calling, "Clumsy? Clumsy! Clumsy?" Brainy helped with the search.

The three Smurfs walked up and down the beach, calling his name.

"Uhhh, a little help here," a small voice called out. "I'm okay . . . I think."

They found Clumsy buried in the sand, being

attacked by crabs, but something was still wrong. Brainy began searching the beach, muttering and flipping out. "My pack! My manual! No! No! No! No!" He dug through a mound of sand. Angry, he turned to face Hefty. "This is all your fault!"

"WHAT?!" Hefty asked, hands on hips, ready to fight.

"Brainy, cut it out!" Smurfette stood with Hefty.

Brainy quickly turned on her. "Oh, I'm sorry. Correction: It's your fault too!"

"Leave her out of this!" Hefty was furious.

"Hefty! I don't need you to fight my fights for me!" Smurfette told him.

"Oh great, so now you're mad at me?" Hefty asked her.

Brainy pointed angrily at Smurfette. "You're the one that got us into this whole mess in the first place!"

"Hey! I was ready to do this on my own," Smurfette shot back, reminding him of how she'd planned to make this journey alone from the beginning.

"Oh, well, then so much for Team Smurf!" Hefty threw up his hands. The gang was breaking up.

"I WANT TO YELL ABOUT SOMETHING!" Clumsy shouted, just to be like the others.

"Stay out of this, Clumsy!" Brainy now turned on him too.

"YELLING!!" Clumsy yelled back.

Hefty couldn't take it any longer. "That's it, Brain Man! It's time for you to earn your manners badge." He charged after Brainy.

"Stop it!" Smurfette tried to break them up, but Brainy lunged at Hefty.

The fight had just begun when suddenly, dozens of arrows rained down on them. *SHWOOP! SHWOOP!*

"Take cover!" Smurfette shouted.

Hefty pulled them all together as they were encircled by a giant caterpillar-like creature that appeared from the bush.

The caterpillar disassembled, coming apart piece by piece. Each part was a small masked creature.

Clumsy fainted, face-first, into the sand.

One of the creatures stepped forward, as though curious. The rest of the creatures prodded the Smurfs forward, forcing them to march. Hefty carried Clumsy in his arms as they left the beach with their captors, who were leading them into the woods.

Team Smurf was terrified. Would they ever get home again?

Suddenly, the creatures stopped. They gathered around the Smurfs with whispers of confusion and excitement.

One creature came closer to them. It felt threatening.

Hefty stepped forward, blocking his friends, trying to keep them safe. Smurfette peeked over his shoulder.

"Who are you? Whaddya want?" Hefty demanded to know.

"Her," the creature said, pointing at Smurfette.

All the masked creatures suddenly rushed up and started grabbing at Smurfette, touching her hair and examining her dress.

"Smurfette!" Hefty tried to push them back, but there were too many of them.

"Hey!" Smurfette batted their hands away.

"Look at that hair," one said.

"And that dress," said another.

"Funny shoes," a third creature laughed.

"She smells good."

"She looks weird."

The creatures went on and on, checking Smurfette out.

Pushing through the crowd, one creature came forward, coming face-to-face with Smurfette. They studied each other for a beat.

The creature was so familiar. . . . Smurfette gasped, "It's you!"

The creature ripped off its mask.

It was a Smurf. A *girl* Smurf. Just like Smurfette!

"You're a girl!" Smurfette jumped for joy and then told her friends, "She's a girl!"

Another creature took off her mask. Then another and another.

"Oh!" Smurfette said as she began to understand that they were *all* girls. "Ohhhhhhhhhh . . ."

"This is her," the first Smurf told the others. "This is the Smurf I was telling you about."

A chorus of whispers rose up from the crowd. "The one from the wall? She's real."

The first Smurf reached forward to pinch Smurfette's skin, examining her closely. "I'm Smurflily."

"Hi. I'm Smurfette," Smurfette replied.

One of the creatures removed her mask and leaped forward, nearly knocking Smurfette over while trying to hug her. "Oh my jeez-to-petes," she apologized. "I'm Smurfblossom. Nice to meet you! We don't have a Smurfette. But we do have . . ." She took a big breath in and pointed at the others. "Smurfpetal, Smurfclover, Smurfmeadow, Smurfdaisy, Smurfholly, Smurfhazel—"

"Heeeey." A group of girls took off their masks and waved.

"Oh, everyone can just introduce themselves later." Smurfblossom waved them away and then spun Smurfette around. "Look at you! You're so different. I mean, sorry, but it's true. Do you know how to start a fire with just a rope and a stick? I do! I can show you. Actually, Smurfstorm can show you; she's the best at that kind of thing. Right, Stormy?"

Smurfstorm was not as enthusiastic about Smurfette as the others. She took aim at the Smurfs with her bow and arrow.

Smurfblossom didn't let Smurfstorm ruin the mood. "That means yes! Have you ever seen a rainbow? What about a double rainbow? What about an upside-down rainbow? So is your favorite song 'Hey, Hey, Hey, Hey, Hey! Hey, Hey, Hey, Hey, Hey, Hey, Hey!'? Mine is. Your dress is sooooooo pretty!"

Smurfette was overwhelmed.

Smurflily told her to calm down. "Smurfblossom, remember, work on that filter, okay?"

Smurfblossom was too wound up for slow breaths. She breathed as fast as she talked.

Smurfstorm was more cautious than her sisters. She leaned forward into Smurfette's face. "What's your deal, anyway?"

"Oh, uh, well . . ." Suddenly, it all came rushing back to Smurfette—the reason for her mission! She had to warn them, to protect them! "We came to warn you about Gargamel!" Smurfette blurted.

"Garga-what?" the girls all asked at once.

"He's a dangerous wizard who wants to capture all Smurfs and use them for his evil magic! And he knows about the lost village."

The girls gave one another a look.

"Lost village?" Smurfstorm fumed. "You're the ones who are lost. Not us."

"We have to take you to Smurfwillow," Smurflily told Smurfette.

Another girl asked about Hefty, Clumsy, and Brainy, saying, "What should we do with these blue blobs?"

Smurflily checked them out, then said, "Oh, ummm . . . bring them along!"

"Come on, Smurfette!" Smurfblossom was so excited about their new friend. "Wait'll you see Smurfy Grove. I'm gonna show you my room, you can tell me all about Gargasmell, and then I can braid your hair. Do you want hear my favorite song again? Hey, hey, hey, hey, hey, hey . . ."

A tough girl Smurf pushed the boys forward. "All right, move!"

Clumsy stumbled on the path. "Wow. Girl Smurfs be bossy."

The Smurfs were led to Smurfy Grove. Trumpets sounded as they approached the entrance. The doors opened, and the members of Team Smurf found themselves looking out over the center of Smurfy Grove, surrounded now by one hundred girl Smurfs who were whispering and chatting.

"Who's the girl and what are those other things?"

"Oh, gross!"

"I think they're kinda cute, in a gross way."

"What are those?"

"The strange ones aren't wearing any shirts."

"I can see their tails!"

"Is there something wrong with them?"

"Are they sick?"

"Are they food?"

Stormy raised her weapon toward the boys.

Smurfette stood up, high on a box, and explained, "No, no, no . . . They're Smurfs. Just like us. Except, well, they're *boy* Smurfs."

"Boy" was a new word, and it quickly spread through the grove, whispered from girl to girl.

"Boy," Smurfblossom repeated it. "That's a funny word. Boy, boy, boy, boy, boy, boy." She lowered her voice like the boys'. "Look at me, I'm a *boy* Smurf. Ha-ha-ha!"

Hefty, Clumsy, and Brainy gave one another a look. They were a little worried about where this was headed.

"Boys?"

"Where do they come from?"

"Ew!"

"So gross!"

"Boys—ick."

"Funny looking."

"Not that smart."

"They smell like soil."

"Sweaty."

"Why are their voices so low?"

"Are those pants attached to shoes or shoes attached to pants?"

"Where's their hair?"

"Where's their shirts?"

"I like what I see!"

"I want to not like them, but I'm somehow drawn to them."

So many voices at once! They were crowding around the boys. One of them poked at Hefty's heart tattoo.

"Brainy's log, day two: We've encountered a rare, new life-form. They are at times very intimidating, and they smell nice. More on that later."

"Hello, boy," one of the girls said, starting to reach for him, but Brainy pushed her back.

"Boundaries! Okay! Ahh! Hey! That's enough of that!"

"They're my friends." Smurfette introduced them. "That's Hefty, Brainy, and Clumsy."

Clumsy waved. "Hey there!"

"Hooptie, Berney, Klutzy. Got it." Smurfblossom really didn't have the names down at all. "We should do name tags!"

"Wait. Where are . . . all your boys?" Smurfette looked around. She hadn't seen any boys in the entire grove. Not yet, anyway.

Giggles filled the air.

"You won't find any boys here." A voice echoed through the square.

Everyone looked up to find a masked creature standing on a balcony high above them. When she removed her mask, she revealed a face that was older, wiser—much like Papa Smurf. She slowly moved down a winding staircase made of vines, like an old lady. But then suddenly she jumped off the side, grabbing on to a spinning flower-copter and landing confidently next to Smurflily.

"I am Smurfwillow, leader of the Smurfs."

Smurfette was in awe.

Smurfwillow nudged her. "This is called an introduction, so now you go."

"Uh . . . I, uh . . . ," Smurfette began.

Smurfstorm stepped in between Smurfwillow

and Team Smurf. "Don't get too close, Willow," Smurfstorm warned. "Something's not right here."

Smurfette jumped in, "I promise, we're only here to help. We came to warn you about the evil wizard Gargamel. He has a map, with a landmark leading him to three tall trees. Show them, Brainy."

"Snappy," Brainy called. Snappy Bug popped out from under Brainy's hat.

Out of caution, Smurfstorm drew her bow and trained it on Snappy. "Don't try any funny stuff, bug."

Snappy took a deep breath, marched past Smurfstorm, and drew the Three Tall Trees in the dirt.

"I hate to break it to you, but those aren't trees," Smurfwillow told them.

Smurfette and the boys walked with Smurfwillow to a place where the view in the distance was clear, and looked out to where Smurfwillow was facing. She was pointing to the lagoon where they'd come from, and above it . . .

"Waterfalls? They're waterfalls!" Smurfette considered the wizard's misunderstanding. "That means Gargamel is going the wrong way!"

"And if he went there"—Smurfwillow gestured toward the Three Tall Trees—"then that means the Swamp of No Return!" Smurfwillow was satisfied they were all safe. "There's no way he could survive."

# Chapter
# 11

In the Swamp of No Return, Gargamel was indeed in deep trouble.

"Help me! Help me! There's no way we can survive!" the wizard shouted into the wind.

With Azrael on his head, Gargamel held on to his bird for dear life as he was attacked by vicious, enchanted piranhas.

Back in Smurfy Grove, Smurfette told Smurfstorm, "With all due respect, you don't know Gargamel." She knew that Gargamel could weasel his way out of even the most dire situations and that it was wrong to underestimate him.

"Yeah? Well, with *no* due respect, you don't know us," Smurfstorm told her.

Smurfblossom agreed. "Trust us, he's a goner!"

Smurfwillow suggested, "Stormy, why don't you

do a little recon, check things out."

"And leave you with these four? No way! Look at that one!" Smurfstorm cried, narrowing her eyes at Hefty. "He can't be normal."

"I think we'll be just fine here," Smurfwillow replied calmly.

With sigh and a sharp whistle, Smurfstorm called "Spitfire!" A Dragonfly zoomed down from the treetops and landed nearby.

Smurfstorm climbed onto Spitfire's back and asked, "Okay, what does this Gargamel look like?"

"Oh, you know," Clumsy replied. "He's your typical male wizard—long black robe, lives alone with his cat and his bird. It's sad, really."

Smurfstorm made a quick decision and nodded toward Clumsy. "You're coming with me. You can point him out."

"Hey! Whoa, whoa, whoa!" Hefty tried to intercede. "There's no way he's getting on—"

But Smurfstorm snatched Clumsy before there could be any further discussion.

"Ahhhhh!" Clumsy shrieked as they lifted off the ground. "I feel the need to remind you, my name is Clumsy." The Dragonfly rose higher into the sky. "WHOOOOOAAAAAA!"

"Clumsy!" Hefty called out as they disappeared over the horizon.

"Don't worry, Clumsy is in good hands," Smurfwillow told him.

Smurfblossom smiled. "Oh, Stormy is the sweetest! . . . In her own way."

Once they were gone, Smurfwillow turned to the girls. "All right, girls, in the meantime, our guests have had a long journey, so let's show them some hospitality, Smurfy Grove style!"

The girl Smurfs cheered and ran off in every direction. They were going to have a party!

Hefty, Brainy, and Smurfette were the center of attention at the welcome celebration.

There was music. Confetti and flower petals floated in the air.

They were given gifts: necklaces, bracelets, beads, feathers, leaves, flower crowns, and ornate head dressings. Hefty was awkward and unsure of all the new things and attention, but Brainy was intrigued by all the customs and different objects in Smurfy Grove. Smurfette was trying her best to take everything in. She was loving every inch of the grove and every minute of her time there.

After the initial celebration was over, Hefty, Brainy, and Smurfette split up to tour the different areas of Smurfy Grove.

In one of the shops, Brainy was explaining a long math problem to the girls, but he couldn't figure out why they were all laughing. It wasn't until he turned around that he saw Hefty drawing a fart cloud on the blackboard behind him.

Later, the girls took Hefty and Brainy to the gym. Hefty was trying his best to impress the girls by lifting the heaviest weights. Suddenly, a fart noise rang out every time he lifted a weight, and the girls broke into laughter. Brainy and Snappy Bug were using a whoopee cushion to get revenge!

Still sour about what happened at the gym, Hefty took a seat in a circle of Smurf girls who were working together to make camouflage leaf quilts. Hefty kept poking himself with the needle as he tried to help; he was irritated but determined to get it right. A few hours later, Hefty's fingers were covered in bandages, but he held up a quilt that was surprisingly detailed and well-done. He smiled . . . until Brainy held up an even bigger quilt of his own.

While Hefty and Brainy were off trying new things, Smurfwillow took Smurfette to the archery range. Smurfette was surprised to find out she was quite good at using a bow and arrow! After archery, Smurfette and some of the other girls went flower jumping. It was a little scary at first, but once she got the hang of it, Smurfette was whirling down the biggest tree in delight. The rest of the day was a blur—Tai Chi, basketball, even Dragonfly riding!

At the end of the day, Smurfwillow showed Smurfette a huge mural of the girl Smurfs. Smiling, Smurfette painted herself into the picture. Her heart was bursting with joy and happiness at the freedom she was experiencing.

Smurfette wasn't sure she'd ever want to leave.

In the depths of the Swamp of No Return, Gargamel was still struggling to get out of the swamp. He grabbed Monty by the tail, demanding, "Flap, Monty! Flap vigorously! Use your mighty condor wings to carry your master to safety!"

A piranha bit Gargamel on the butt.

"OUCH! Sweet mercy! They're bottom-feeders!

Ouch! Ah! Ah!" Gargamel grabbed one of the piranhas and decided to teach it a lesson. "Devil fish!"

Azrael noticed there were Smurfs flying above them. "Mreow!"

Gargamel slammed the piranha into the ground, then yelled to Azrael, "WHERE. IS. MY. LOST. SMURF. VILLAGE?!"

"Mreow!" the cat answered.

Gargamel looked up. "What?" High above them, he saw Smurfstorm and Clumsy. "Smurfs! Why won't they just die?! Monty, retrieve them!" Gargamel commanded his bird.

Monty flapped away to chase down Smurfstorm and Clumsy.

From far above, Smurfstorm and Clumsy hadn't seen Monty yet. They were still searching for Gargamel. Suddenly, Spitfire made a jerky swoop, causing Clumsy to hold on tight.

Clumsy was busy still trying to explain to Smurfstorm about the wizard. "Oh, he exists all right. He and his stinky cat and his doo-doo bird. They've been terrorizing us the entire journey. But he didn't like us from the start.

"He could never find our village," Clumsy

continued. "So then he made a plan to capture us all. That's when Gargamel created Smurfette. Anyways—"

Smurfstorm hadn't really been paying much attention to Clumsy's rambling, but that last tidbit of information made her pause. "Hold up! Smurfette was created by this Gargamel?"

"Oh, yeah. From a lump of clay. Really cool story, actually." Clumsy smiled.

"I knew I didn't trust her." Smurfstorm frowned.

"You'd like her if you get to know her. She's just like you but nice," Clumsy said, about to go on when Smurfstorm noticed Monty flying toward them.

"Hold on! We gotta bogey coming in."

That made no sense to Clumsy. Smurfstorm reached out and physically turned his head so he could see Monty, headed straight for them.

"That's no bogey! That's Gargamel's big dumb bird!" Clumsy said, panic rising inside him.

"Here, you fly." She pushed the Dragonfly reins toward Clumsy.

"Uhhh, that's not a great idea," Clumsy said. "Flying's not really my thing."

"Have you ever flown before?" Smurfstorm asked.

"Well, no . . . ," Clumsy admitted.

"Then how do you know it's not your thing?" Before he could protest again, Smurfstorm shoved the reins into his hands while she fired off shots with her bow and arrow. Through sheer dumb luck, Monty was able to avoid the arrows.

"He's coming back!" Smurfstorm warned Clumsy.

She had a stash of ammo ready to fire: berries, sticks, and rocks. But she would run out if they didn't shake the bird soon. "Hurry!" she told Clumsy.

"Uhhh. What do I do?" He had no idea what she meant. Accidentally, he caused the Dragonfly to swerve, just in time to dodge Monty's attack.

"Good move! Now, do it again!" Smurfstorm cheered.

"Oooookaaayyy . . ." Clumsy wasn't sure he could do it again, but he was willing to try. With a tug on the reins, he managed to get Spitfire to spiral expertly into the air. "Hee-haw!" he cheered.

But Monty was still hot on their tail.

Having freed himself from the swamp, Gargamel was now standing at the murky water's edge, staring up at Clumsy. "Yeeessss!" Then he realized something important. "Wait a minute! I don't recognize that other Smurf!" He gasped. "It's a girl! They found my lost Smurf village!"

Clumsy ducked and dove the Dragonfly away from Monty. He passed another arrow to Spitfire. "Hey! I've got an idea! Spitfire, spit fire!"

Spitfire lit up the end of the arrow with flames, and Clumsy handed it back to Smurfstorm.

"I like the way you think," she said. She took the shot and hit Monty's wing.

"Ouch, ouch, ouch, ouch," Monty squawked, then fell out of the sky, injured. Gargamel ran to catch him.

"Monty!! What have they done to you my glorious bird of prey?" Gargamel shook his fist up at the Dragonfly. "SMMMUUUURRRRFFFSSSS!!!!!!"

"I can't believe he escaped the swamp! We have to warn the others!" Smurfstorm set a course for home.

"You hear that, Spitfire? Back to Smurfy Grove," Clumsy said, anxious to get as far away from Gargamel as possible.

Unaware of the danger approaching the grove, Hefty and Brainy were relaxing in a Smurf-spa. Hefty was wearing an organic facial mask. A caterpillar began using its many legs to give him a back massage.

"So . . . interesting day," Brainy said, looking over at his friend.

"Yeah," Hefty said happily.

"*You* actually did math," Brainy said.

"Not just math . . . *basic* math," Hefty bragged.

Above them, there was a rustling sound as Smurfette floated down to them on a daisy.

"Hey, guys! Isn't this place awesome?!" She looked radiant and happy, decked out in traditional Smurfy Grove clothing.

She was hanging out with Smurfblossom and a few other girl Smurfs.

"Doesn't she look great? It's like she's one of us now!" Smurfblossom said with a huge smile. "She should stay with us forever!"

Smurfblossom's words hit Hefty like a punch in the gut. He didn't want Smurfette to stay with them! She belonged with her friends in Smurf Village!

"Uhhh, one, she always looks great," he said. Then adding, "Two, this is gettin' a little outta hand, don't you think?"

Smurfette giggled. "Sorry. I can't take you seriously with that mask on your face."

Hefty yanked off the beads and feathered hat he was wearing and wiped his face.

Brainy slowly began to clean himself up too.

Hefty stood. "Smurfette, we did what we came here to do. These Smurfs know about Gargamel, so come on, let's start thinking about heading home." Despite himself, a bit of panic snuck into Hefty's voice. It was time to leave before they lost Smurfette to Smurfy Grove forever.

"Home? But I . . ." Smurfette looked around at the village and the girl Smurfs who surrounded her. It was so perfect.

"He's right, Smurfette. We've been gone almost two whole days. Papa Smurf's going to be very upset with us," Brainy said, reminding her where they really belonged.

"It's time to go," Hefty added.

104

Smurfette was quiet for a long moment.

"Smurfette!" Hefty said to get her full attention. Just then a whirring noise made them all look up.

"Incoming Dragonfly!" Clumsy announced from high in the sky. His friends stared in amazement as Clumsy explained, "Turns out—I *do* do well with Dragonflies."

Smurfstorm was all business as she slid confidently off the Dragonfly and marched right up to Smurfette, who was standing with Smurfwillow.

"They were right. This Gargamel character . . . He's real, and he's headed this way," Smurfstorm told them all.

"Oh no! See, I told you—" Smurfette began, but she was cut off by Smurfstorm.

"Put a cork in it, Smurfette. The way I see it, you and your little boy friends led him straight to us. But of course, that was your plan all along, wasn't it?"

"Smurfstorm, easy—" Clumsy protested.

Smurfstorm turned to the crowd, as though she were a lawyer presenting her case. "Little Miss Yellow Hair here isn't a real Smurf. She was created by Gargamel. The Clumsy blob told me so himself."

Smurfwillow put up a hand. "Smurfette, is this true?"

"I— It's not like that." Smurfette wanted to defend herself.

"She was made to help him find Smurfs!" Smurfstorm's eyes were filled with anger.

"Smurfette came here to help you. We all did," Hefty put in.

"It's okay, Hefty. This is all my fault." Smurfette looked around sadly. She'd been so happy here, and now things were turning ugly.

Just then, the village alarm sounded. The ear-piercing wail screeched through the town.

"Girls! Protection mode!" Smurfwillow commanded. The girl Smurfs disappeared into their homes and returned a moment later with weapons.

They stood, tense and ready, as a rustling sound came from the nearby bushes.

"Hold!" Smurfwillow told them, commanding her troops. "Hold!"

Suddenly, a blaze of red, blue, and green light burst through the leaves!

"NOW!" Smurfwillow leaped forward and attacked the intruder, pinning him to a tree.

# Chapter 12

Smurfwillow had captured Papa Smurf. He'd come into the village riding on Bucky the Glow-Bunny.

Papa managed to break free and face his attacker. She was wielding a staff. But Papa had mean fighting skills. They were evenly matched. The battle between them went on and on until Smurfwillow stepped into a pool of light, allowing Papa to see that she was a Smurf!

For a second, he was so surprised that he was thrown off guard. That gave Smurfwillow time to take the lead and defeat him.

"Surrender, wizard!" she demanded.

"Wiz— What? Who are—?" Papa had no idea who he was facing or what she meant.

Girl Smurfs began to slowly emerge from behind trees and rocks. Papa was stunned.

The girls checked him out.

"Oh, he's so old," one said.

"Look at his face." Another leaned in close.

"Is he wearing a disguise?" A girl reached out toward Papa's beard.

"He doesn't seem so tough," Smurfstorm said with a hearty laugh.

"Yeah, Gargamel! That's what you get when you attack Smurfy Grove!" Smurfblossom shouted, doing a happy victory dance.

"Gargamel? What are you—?" Papa didn't understand.

Smurfette worked her way through the crowd. "Wait! This is a mistake!"

"Smurfette?!" He was already confused. Now it was worse. What was she doing here?

"That's Papa!" Smurfette told the group.

"Papa? There's another funny word," Smurf-blossom rolled the word around on her tongue. "Papa, Papa, Paaaaapaaaaa!" Feeling satisfied that she got it right, and also that he was the bad guy, she raised her stick, preparing to charge at him.

"Smurfblossom! No!" Smurfwillow shouted.

Smurflily stepped in and snatched Smurfblossom's stick away.

"Oh, come on! Just give me one good hit!" Smurfblossom was all wound up.

"Breathe deep and step away from the Papa thing," Smurfwillow told her.

Smurfette stood next to Papa and introduced him. "Everyone . . . meet Papa Smurf."

Excited whispers filled the air as the girls surrounded Papa, pulling on his beard and poking at him. They were talking so fast, he couldn't always see who was saying what:

"Hi."

"I'm Smurfjade."

"How old are you?"

"Are you a wizard?"

"What's that thing on your face?"

"How does it stay on?"

Papa's head was spinning so he pushed away from them to get some air. "There's so many. . . ." He leaned over to Smurfette and asked her, "Where are the boys?"

Hefty, Clumsy, and Brainy stepped forward. They knew they were in big trouble.

Hefty kicked the dirt, not wanting to make eye contact. "'Sup, Papa."

Brainy looked down too. "Hello there."

Only Clumsy was excited to see Papa. He blurted out, "I rode a Dragonfly!"

Papa was angry that they'd left the village, but he was also glad to see them. "Well, thank goodness you're all okay."

Papa then turned to Smurfwillow. Finding out that there were other female Smurfs . . . This was the biggest surprise of his long life.

"How did you find us?" Smurfette asked. She hadn't left any clues to where she was going.

"I, uh, wasn't born yesterday, you know," he told her, which made Smurfwillow laugh.

"That's clear," she said as a small joke.

Papa ignored her, telling his Smurfs, "Look. You four are coming home with me. Now." He pointed to the waiting bunny.

"Not so fast, Papa thing." Smurfwillow blocked his way.

"Papa thi—? I— Are you the one in charge around here?" He was insulted.

"That's right," she said. "I'm Smurfwillow. Leader of the Smurfs."

"Well, I'm afraid that's quite impossible, because

I happen to be the leader of the Smurfs, so—"

Smurfwillow rolled her eyes. "Whatever you say, Papa thing."

Papa was trying his best to be civil, but she was making him mad. "Excuse me? Do you mind not calling me that?"

"Well, if the thing fits . . ." Smurfwillow was still standing directly in front of Papa. The two of them stared at each other, hard.

Finally, Papa asked, "By the way. Where'd you learn those moves?"

"Self taught, actually," she said, not turning her gaze.

"Impressive." Papa gave a small nod.

"Thank you," she replied.

"You're quite welcome."

They smiled slightly at each other and then bowed. None of the Smurfs in the grove understood what was going on between them.

Smurfette cut in, asking, "Okay, not sure what's happening here, but, uh, what about Gargamel?"

"Now what's all this nonsense about Garga—?" Papa started when all of a sudden there was a *BOOM!*

And a FLASH!

When the burst of green smoke cleared, Papa and Smurfwillow were stuck like statues. They'd been hit by one of Gargamel's Freeze Balls!

"Gargamel!" Smurfette shouted, looking around frantically. Where was he hiding?

"Oh, I'm sorry, did I scare you?" Gargamel chuckled, stepping out into the open. "I hope so."

He grabbed Papa Smurf and Smurfwillow and threw them into a sack.

Smurfette called out, "Everybody, run!"

That made Gargamel laugh even harder. There would be no escape. "Prepare for Garmageddon!" he told them all.

POUNCE! Azrael crashed through the grove, blocking their path, while Monty zoomed over-head. The bird pushed anyone who wanted to leave back toward Azrael.

They were trapped.

Smurfs took off in every direction, running for whatever cover they could find.

"Spears, now!" Smurfstorm commanded.

Some of the girls got ready to throw spears at Gargamel, but the wizard wasn't scared. "Gargamel says 'freeze'!" he shouted, blowing freeze powder on the attacking Smurfs.

Gargamel clapped with joy when the Smurfs stopped moving. "That's right! Smurf tested, Gargamel approved, grade A, first-class high-octane Freeze Balls!"

He attacked again, and this time Smurfstorm was frozen.

"Freeze Ball! Freeze Ball! Freeze Ball!" Gargamel chanted as he tossed them at the Smurfs.

"Mreow, mreow, mreow!" Azrael complained.

"Well, I assume they'll still work if I don't shout 'Freeze Ball,'" Gargamel explained. "But we'll never know." He tossed another toward a group of fleeing Smurfs. "Freeze Ball!"

Monty helped Gargamel with an aerial attack, dropping Freeze Balls from overhead.

Smurfette tried desperately to save her new friends. She dashed from Smurf to Smurf, trying to shake them out of it.

Gargamel took aim directly at Smurfette, but Hefty jumped in front of her. "Smurfette!"

Hefty was frozen.

"Hefty?!" Smurfette tried to break the spell

while Gargamel tossed dozens of stunned Smurfs into his sack.

"It's. Over. Smurfette." Hefty struggled to get out each word.

Gargamel was thrilled, dancing around, scooping up Smurfs as though he were putting jelly beans into a jar.

Azrael held open the bag. "Meow!"

Gargamel called to the bird, "Monty! Bag o' Smurfs!"

Monty swooped down and picked up the sack with his beak.

Smurfette was the only one not frozen. She desperately tried to break Hefty free of his stun spell. Or Brainy. Or Clumsy. Anybody.

Hefty mumbled through frozen lips, "It's time. For you. To run."

As he finished, Gargamel snatched Hefty and Brainy.

"NO!" Smurfette shrieked.

"Two more for pick up!" Gargamel tossed Brainy and Hefty into the air, and Monty scooped them up. The bird headed into the darkness. Gargamel laughed. "Ha, ha, ha, ha, ha!"

Smurfette was devastated.

Gargamel turned around to face her. "Ah, Smurfette, my little creation!" he cooed. "You finally did what you were made for."

"No, it's not true," she cried, refusing to believe him.

"Of course it is! Why do you think you led me here? Why did you save me on the river?" He gave her a wicked grin. "It was all part of the plan. No matter how hard you try, you can't escape your destiny. But now you're really of no use to me anymore." He reached into his bag, said "Freeze Ball," then tossed his last one at her.

Smurfette was frozen and helpless.

"Thank you for everything," Gargamel told her, then grabbed the last of the girl Smurfs.

Smurfblossom, with tears in her eyes, fought to say, "Smurfette, how could you do this to us?"

Gargamel grabbed her and said, "Because it was her purpose!" And then he took off.

Smurfette was stuck: frozen and all alone.

It was over.

Smurfy Grove was empty.

Gargamel had captured all the Smurfs.

And it was all Smurfette's fault.

# Chapter 13

When the freezing spell wore off, Smurfette crumpled to the ground. She was scared. Her tears turned to sobs just as rain began to fall.

Gargamel never froze Brainy's Snappy Bug, but in the fighting, he'd gotten flipped over on his back. He wiggled and squirmed his way back onto his feet and scurried over to Smurfette. Snappy Bug was worried. In an attempt to lift Smurfette's spirits, he drew a heart in the mud, but that only made Smurfette cry harder.

The Dragonfly Spitfire rested nearby. He was also worried about Smurfette.

Out of the darkness, Bucky, the Glow-Bunny, appeared in the clearing.

Smurfette looked up through her tears and said, "Huh?"

Snappy Bug jumped at the opportunity to show Smurfette something to cheer her up. She quickly printed the smurfy selfie of Smurfette and the boys around the campfire, in much happier times.

Smurfette gazed at the selfie, longing for her friends. Then she turned away. "I'm sorry, you guys. . . ." She was too sad to think about anything.

Snappy Bug nuzzled against her, giving her a bug hug. Spitfire and Bucky joined them. Bucky gave her a little nudge, as if to say, "You can do it. Go get them!"

Smurfette sighed. "No, Snappy. I've done too much damage already."

Snappy played a recording of their journey. It started with Hefty's voice: "We're Team Smurf, and we're in this together."

Then Smurfette was heard: "We're Smurfs. We do the right thing."

Smurfette thought about the recoding, their journey, and everything that had happened.

"I'm not even a real Smurf," she cried. Then she stopped crying, as though she'd realized something. "I'm not a real Smurf!"

Suddenly, she jumped up, grabbed Snappy Bug,

and climbed onto Bucky's back.

They took off!

At Gargamel's lair, the sky was dark and ominous. It was raining. Thunder crashed. Lightning lit up the sky.

"We need more power!" the wizard called to Monty.

Gargamel pulled a lever on a giant contraption. "Faster, Monty, faster! Yes."

A cookie dropped in front of Monty, who was running on a treadmill that powered the machine. Monty ran as fast as his little bird legs could handle while Gargamel inspected the different parts of the machine.

"The jiggler is jiggling. The spin-y thing is spinning. The smoke is going up." It was working! "The bubblers are bubbling. Hubbuda, hubbuda! Perfect!"

All the power flowed into a clear fishbowl-shaped centrifuge. It began to swirl and bubble.

Gargamel examined the bowl with glee. "Ooooh! It's almost there."

The Smurfs were trapped in cages hanging from the rafters. In one cage, Brainy attempted to pick the lock with his hand while Hefty and Smurfstorm waited, hoping he could free them.

"Here's what we're going to do," Brainy said. "I pick this lock. . . ."

"Yeah?" Hefty, Clumsy, and Smurfstorm chorused.

"We swing to that shelf. . . ." Brainy pointed out a shelf on the far side of the room.

"Yeah?"

"Pick up something heavy . . ."

"Yeah?"

"And use it to kill the bird!" Brainy finished.

"Wait! You want us to kill the bird?!" Hefty asked incredulously.

"Fine," Brainy conceded. "We'll just knock him unconscious."

The others agreed to this plan while Smurfstorm made some hand signals to Smurfwillow, who was in another cage with Papa. "They have an escape plan. But they're going to need our help."

"It's time to rock the cage," Papa said.

Smurfwillow gave him a look. "Don't be weird."

Across the room, Brainy gave the lock one more twist and *click*! It opened. They all linked hands and leaped from the cages. Hefty held on as they swung over to the next cage like trapeze artists. Papa and Smurfwillow grabbed hold, and they continued to form links with their hands. "Gotcha!" Smurfwillow shouted.

Azrael spotted them and meowed to get Gargamel's attention, "MEOW! MEOW!!!"

Gargamel scowled at his cat. "Stop that, Azrael! I can't calibrate my machine with all your incessant yammering!"

Papa and Smurfwillow, meanwhile, swung the Smurfs over to the nearby shelf, making a chain with Hefty and Clumsy at its front. Gargamel turned and saw the string of Smurfs that were practically free. "Sweet mercy! It's another jail-break! Azrael! You're completely useless." With that, the wizard swooped them up in his net, breaking the chain and leaving Hefty and Brainy alone on the shelf. "Lucky for you I have eyes in the back of my head."

"No, Gargamel! No!" Papa yelled.

"Quiet down! You'll all get your turn! In you

go!" Gargamel dumped the Smurfs from his net into the centrifuge, and they started to spin, the color draining from them as they spun around.

Gargamel was completely focused on the spinning centrifuge, studying the fluid closely as its color began to glow brighter. A blue mist rose up from the centrifuge and flowed into the machine. Gargamel smiled and turned a handle; the magic descended upon him in a glowing display.

Smurfwillow and Papa rattled the bars of their cage. "NOOOOOO!"

"Yes! That's the stuff! Ha, ha, ha! It's working! I can feel it! I can feel the power!" Gargamel used his new power to give himself a wizard makeover, starting with his robe.

"Oh-ho, ho, ho, ho!" New clean robes appeared. Next, he touched his head and *ZAAAAP!* A full head of luxurious hair grew.

"Ha, ha, ha! Check out my wizard mane!" Gargamel shook his long hair delightedly.

"When I'm through with these Smurfs, I'll have all the power I've ever dreamed of!"

Smurfette stepped out of the shadows. "Almost all the power!"

Hefty ran to one side of the cage. "Smurfette!" he cried out.

Gargamel's grin grew. "Smurfette?! What a lovely surprise. Are you done crying in the woods?" He zapped a bolt of energy at her.

She slid down a curtain. "I've shed enough tears for these Smurfs!"

Gargamel looked at her with interest. "What's this?"

Smurfette continued, "I'm done pretending to be something I'm not. I've come to repledge my loyalty to you! My true papa!"

# Chapter 14

Papa and Smurfwillow were watching Smurfette from their cage.

"She can't be serious?" Smurfwillow asked Papa.

"No, no, no," Papa assured her. "She would never!"

"Oh Smurfette," Gargamel said. "Even if I did believe you—which I don't!—what could you possibly offer me that I don't already have? A tiny little massage that I can't even feel?"

Smurfette had her answer ready. "How about the rest of the Smurfs?"

Gargamel laughed as if she'd just told him the funniest joke. "Yeah, right." Then he considered her offer. "Wait, what?"

"Just think of all the power you'll have once I reveal the location of Smurf Village," she told him.

Gargamel was suddenly interested. "Let's see, now . . . One hundred more Smurfs . . . That's ten times the power. No, sixteen times the . . . Let's see, carry the one . . ." He gave up on doing the math. "Whatever! It's a lot more power! Now, why are you doing this?"

"I'm so tired of being good," Smurfette said. "Use your power to transform me back to my evil self."

"Your loyalty has returned to you." The wizard was pleased.

"So do we have a deal?" Smurfette asked.

The Smurfs in cages gasped. Papa yelled, "Smurfette, no!"

"Quiet, you vile blue rats, I'm thinking! Okay, I'm done! Let's do it!" Gargamel let his power build and threw every bit of it at her. "One evil Smurfette, coming right up!" He zapped her with power and held the magical beam steady.

Smurfette focused on the power and began to emit a bright light. The glow acted like a force field against the magic. It was taking all her strength to stay steady.

Hefty and Brainy watched, uncertain of what

she was doing, when Brainy said, "Wait! Of course!"

"Wait!" Gargamel realized something was wrong. "What's happening? No! No! What are you doing?!"

"Yeah!" Brainy and Hefty cheered. "Go, Smurfette!"

Gargamel's head of thick hair faded away. His robes were reduced back to their original form. His hovel began to fall apart. The machine sparked, overloaded, and shattered.

As the magic deflected off Smurfette, blue coloring returned to the first Smurfs who had gone into the machine.

"NOOOOOOOOO!" Gargamel shouted.

The Smurfs hooted and hollered in celebration.

"Azrael!" Gargamel called to his cat. "Help!! More power!" Azrael ran to turn a dial on the machine, hoping to replenish the wizard's power.

Brainy turned to Hefty. "What are we going to do?"

Hefty spotted a spoon and got an idea. Grabbing Brainy's arm, he pulled him in. "We smurfboard!"

They grabbed the spoon and leaped off the shelf. Together, they smurfboarded down an ax handle, jumped onto a wooden ramp, and launched themselves at Gargamel's bird, Monty. Shouting "TEAM SMURF!" they knocked out Monty, landed, and skidded to a stop. The machine, meanwhile, started sparking and overloading, and then shut down.

A magical tempest began to swirl around the room. As it grew stronger, it shot Gargamel, Azrael, and Monty through the roof!

"Nooooo!" Gargamel screamed as he went flying.

All the Smurfs cheered and shouted Smurfette's name. They hugged one another and danced to celebrate. The Smurfs were saved!

The Smurfs still in cages were set free. They climbed down ladders into the room. The ones in the cauldron woke up to discover their color and magic had returned.

"I'm okay! Yeah!" Clumsy said as Hefty and Brainy helped him up.

"I thought we were goners," Smurfblossom said, embracing her friends.

"Okay, everybody's . . . Thanks goodness," Smurfwillow said, sighing with relief.

"I can't believe she did it!" Brainy said, looking around.

"Where's Smurfette?" Hefty noticed they hadn't seen her.

Smurfette was on a ledge a few feet away, but something wasn't right. As the Smurfs approached, they realized that Gargamel's magic had returned her to her original form—a clay mold of a girl Smurf. She lay in a heap on the ground. The selfie of her and her friends lay next to her.

"Smurfette?" Hefty didn't understand. Was this really her?

Papa Smurf fell to his knees, tears filling his eyes.

Hefty asked, "What happened?" As he said it, his heart ached with sadness.

Papa Smurf explained, "This is what she once was."

All the Smurfs were stunned and very, very sad.

Smurfblossom burst into tears.

Brainy stood there, unable to think for the first time in his life. He felt cold inside.

Suddenly, Papa jumped up and started flipping through Gargamel's spell book. "There has to be something I can do!" He muttered to himself as he flipped pages, "There must be a spell or . . . Where is it? What page? Must be here . . . No, that's not it. Which spell? Which spell?"

The Smurfs watched, feeling powerless. There was no way to help.

Papa anxiously flipped through Gargamel's spell book, searching for an answer.

The Smurfs had tears in their eyes watching Papa. He was desperate to save his little girl.

Brainy stepped forward. "Papa," he said softly. "We won't find the answer to this in a book."

Papa knew that Brainy was right. He slammed the book to the ground, angry and frustrated.

Hefty cradled the clay Smurfette in his arms. "Let's take her home."

# Chapter 15

All the Smurfs, boys and girls, escorted Smurfette home. The woods were peaceful after the rains. Wind whistled through the trees, and the night stars provided a soft glow.

Smurfette's clay form lay in the middle of a circle formed by the Smurfs. The entire village took turns placing flowers and gifts near her, including the selfie of her and the boys.

Papa Smurf stood before the others and said, "Smurfette never believed she was a real Smurf, but she was the truest Smurf of all."

Brainy removed his glasses to wipe his tears. Snappy Bug climbed onto his shoulder. The bug was also crying.

Hefty placed a small bluebell flower on the clay form, holding back his tears.

Clumsy joined his brothers. He took Hefty's hand. The Smurfs began taking one another's hands, until a chain of two hundred Smurfs, from both the village and the grove, surrounded Smurfette.

The wind picked up, and the moon shone brightly, peeking out from behind the clouds.

After a few moments, Smurfs began to break away from the circle to head back to their mushrooms. At last, the only three remaining were Hefty, Brainy, and Clumsy. They stood together, eyes closed, holding hands, bonded forever.

They didn't notice it, but the bluebell flower resting on the clay form began to sparkle.

Slowly but surely, blue light seeped into Smurfette's clay form. Life began to return to her. Smurfette's nose wiggled. Her hair shone golden. And finally, she opened her eyes.

She sat up. "Why is everyone crying?"

Clumsy still had his eyes closed when he responded. "It's Smurfette. She's a lump of clay."

Smurfette stepped close. "No, Clumsy, it's me. I'm right here."

Clumsy looked up to see Smurfette. He grabbed her nose to make sure she was real, then, once convinced, he announced, "Smurfette?! It's Smurfette!"

Brainy and Hefty were still in the moment with their eyes closed.

"Quiet, Clumsy," Brainy said.

"Let him be, Brainy. We all grieve in our own way," Papa said, having returned.

"Clumsy, would you— Oh . . ." Brainy saw Smurfette standing there.

She was awake! The boys all rushed to her side.

Their celebration was so loud that the other Smurfs came running back. Papa Smurf was more stunned than anyone. Smurfette laughed and hugged him tight.

"Look at you. You never cease to amaze me," Papa said. They held each other for a long moment.

When Smurfblossom found out what had happened, she rushed forward, barreling into Smurfette. Then the others joined her, surrounding Smurfette with love and hugs.

Papa Smurf sat in his comfortable chair in his mushroom house. A book lay open on his lap.

"Hey, there . . . Me again. Kind of a wild ride, wasn't it? But in the end, Smurfette found her purpose and united us all."

All two hundred Smurfs were working side by side.

"Let's get two lead welders up on the top!" Handy Smurf called. Smurfette jumped onto a roof with another Smurf.

Clumsy tried to help, but he ended up just tripping. "I'm okay!"

Papa said, "Every Smurf pitched in. We all worked together to rebuild Smurfy Grove, bigger and better than ever."

Smurfwillow and Papa Smurf continued to fight, but now in a ring, with Smurf judges.

"From that day forward, both villages had an open-door policy, and I'm happy to report we see one another often," Papa reported.

Papa Smurf practiced some steps Smurfwillow taught him.

"Pretty good, for an old-timer." Smurfwillow gave him a pat on the back.

"You're not bad yourself," Papa replied with a laugh.

Smurfette helped Brainy in the lab and Baker in the kitchen.

Papa went on reading from his book. "And as for that burning question, what exactly is a Smurfette? Well, it's just a name. It doesn't define her. Smurfette can be whatever she wants to be. But don't take my word for it. . . ."

"What's a Smurfette?" Brainy asked. "Well, I don't need a book to tell you she's—"

"Beeedeeebeeedeeebeee," Snappy interrupted.

"Yes, Snappy, I know. That's exactly what I was going to—"

"Beeedeeebeeedeeebeee," Snappy cut in again.

"Well, if you'd let me finish—"

"Beeedeeebeeedeeebeee."

"Right. Smurfette can't be defined by just one word. She's many things."

"She doesn't know it yet, but she's my new best friend!" Smurfblossom added.

"Smurfette is fearless," Clumsy put in.

"Hmm, well, why don't you tell me what *you* know first," Nosey said.

Hefty catapulted Nosey Smurf into the distance. "Smurfette is *everything*. And more."

"She's tough," Smurfstorm said. "Not as tough as me, but tough."

Paranoid Smurf quickly pulled down the shade and refused to answer.

"Smurfette is a true leader," Smurfwillow put in.

Papa Smurf smiled. "She shines!"

Baker Smurf had one thing to say. "She still stinks at baking!"

Smurfette sat on a bench, watching the usual goings-on in Smurf Village. Everything was back to normal. Jazzy Smurf played his music in the center of town. Grouchy walked up and sat beside her.

"Hey! I'm grouchin' here," Smurfette told him with a frown.

Grouchy was shocked and slinked away.

Smurfette laughed. "Just kidding!"

Grouchy came back, a bit confused, and took his place on his bench. He was really grumpy. "Why don't you go and Smurfette somewhere else?!"

Smurfette flashed him a sweet smile.

"Or, uh . . . I g-guess you can Smurfette right here," he stammered.

Smurfette gave him a big hug. "That's exactly what I intend to do!"

134

Smurfette bounced away, happy and cheerful.

Grouchy watched her go, privately smiling to himself.

All the Smurfs gathered in the center of town. Snappy Bug was ready for them.

"Come on, everyone! Smurfy selfie time!" Smurfette stood in the middle of her two hundred best friends.

All the Smurfs smiled and in one voice said:

"BLUE CHEESE!"

The End . . .